"We met when you... graced my table."

"Oh. Oh, yes." There was a catch in Cicely's throat as she recognized the husky British voice.

"I wonder if you'd have dinner with me," he went on. "Tomorrow night or—"

"I...well..." For a moment she was speechless. Men seldom—almost never— asked her out. And now this man she'd just...well, not even met, was calling her. She gripped the receiver more tightly, remembering how he'd kissed her—a light, casual touch, but it had left her senses reeling.

"Well?" he prompted.

"I don't go out on dates." This was such an embarrassing truth that she hastened to add, "With men I meet on the street."

He gave a low chuckle. "But we didn't meet on the street. We met in a perfectly respectable restaurant."

"My mother would call that 'the street'!"

Eva Rutland, American author, lives in California where she and her husband, retired from the U.S. government, are active in community affairs. She began writing seriously while her four children were growing up. Her articles in top women's magazines were developed into a book, *The Trouble with Being a Mama*. Since then she has had an inspirational romance published, written a musical comedy and had some skits produced on radio and television. Readers will enjoy the warmth, humor and sensitivity in the writing of this new author in the Harlequin Romance series.

Books by Eva Rutland

HARLEQUIN ROMANCE
2897—TO LOVE THEM ALL

Don't miss any of our special offers. Write to us at the following address for information on our newest releases.

Harlequin Reader Service
901 Fuhrmann Blvd., P.O. Box 1397, Buffalo, NY 14240
Canadian address: P.O. Box 603,
Fort Erie, Ont. L2A 5X3

At First Sight

Eva Rutland

Harlequin Books

TORONTO • NEW YORK • LONDON
AMSTERDAM • PARIS • SYDNEY • HAMBURG
STOCKHOLM • ATHENS • TOKYO • MILAN

ISBN 0-373-02944-6

Harlequin Romance first edition November 1988

CHAPTER ONE

SHE KNEW she had returned to the wrong table the minute the man spoke. But by that time, she was already seated in the chair he had pulled out for her, and she'd eased her right foot out of the shoe that was killing her.

"How nice of you to join me." The voice was deep and husky, and the accent decidedly British.

Cicely hardly listened. Her mind whirled helplessly around two inescapable facts. She had no idea where her table was, and she should never have left home without her glasses.

"I'm sorry. Please excuse me." She leaned toward him, trying to focus. His face floated indiscernibly before her, but she thought he had light hair. Certainly not fiery red like Brick Spencer, who was waiting for her at his table and must surely be wondering why she hadn't returned.

"Listen. I made a mistake."

"An extremely pleasant one indeed. I was contemplating a very lonely evening."

Good heavens! Did he think she was one of those women who deliberately set out to pick up strange men?

"You don't understand. I came to the wrong table." The soft conversation of other diners hummed in her ears, and she glanced nervously at the indistinguishable people around her. She should never have left Spencer's table. But the ladies' room was a necessity, so when she'd heard a woman nearby say "Please excuse me. I'll be right back." Cicely had jumped up and followed her. Coming out of the ladies' room, she must have made a wrong turn. "Look," she said to the man before her. "I . . . I have a vision problem."

"With those eyes! I wouldn't have guessed." He leaned closer to peer at her. "Jet black hair and deep blue eyes—a stunning combination!"

For a moment Cicely was left speechless. She had never in her life been called stunning. Maybe this whole charade was going to work. Now if she could just get back to Spencer's table . . .

"Please. If you could just direct me." Her foot groped for the shoe, which had slipped away from her. "To my table, I mean. The gentleman I'm with has very red hair, and he's wearing . . ." Her voice trailed off. Without her glasses she didn't really know what he was wearing. "He's tall and . . . and his suit is dark." Dark brown, or blue, or maybe even black. She wasn't sure. This morning when he passed her in the hotel lobby, he'd worn a light suit. He was a strikingly handsome man; she'd had her glasses on and had seen him clearly, even though she caught only a quick glimpse before George rushed her out. A flash of the irritation she felt then returned to her now.

"Just what is your vision problem?" the man asked.

"I'm very nearsighted." Cicely still groped for her shoe. "Could you please direct me?"

"Nearsighted? But surely glasses—"

"I do have glasses. I left them . . . somewhere." In George's pocket. Because he'd said "They spoil the whole effect." And when she complained that she couldn't see, he had told her to *cling*, that Spencer liked clinging women. And now . . . Dear heaven! How long had she been away? "Please. I have to get back to my table. This is important. A matter of life and death."

"I hate that expression. Life and death! As if they were one and the same. They're complete opposites. Life—"

"I didn't ask for a lecture!" she snapped, then checked herself, trying to restrain her angry frustration. "I just want directions. If you would—"

"My dear lady, you chose to join me. And when I try to engage you in interesting conversation...oh, excuse me! Would you like a glass of wine?"

"I didn't choose! And I don't want any wine. And you are deliberately being obstinate. You're enjoying my predicament. I'll bet you're one of those people who like to see others suffer. I'll bet you park in places reserved for the handicapped. I'll bet—"

"Oh, no indeed. My sympathies are always with the handicapped. But your problem, I'm afraid, is vanity."

"Vanity!" She stared at his blurred image. No one had ever accused her of being vain; in fact, her mother always said she wasn't vain enough.

"Can you deny that you purposely left your glasses at home in order to appear more beautiful?" She heard the laughter in his voice and flushed.

"Never mind," she said. "I'll try to manage by myself. If you would just be kind enough to find my shoe and push it over to me—"

He laughed out loud at that. "Dear me! Do you mean to say you left your shoe somewhere, too?"

"No. It's my mother's shoe, and she wears a half size smaller, and..." She stopped. Why was she explaining to this man? "Oh, will you stop laughing and just get the shoe for me."

"Perhaps I'd better," he said, and obliged. But Cicely's relief as her foot made contact with the elusive shoe was shattered by his next words. "I can see the man you described glaring at us from across the room."

"Oh, my goodness!" Cicely jammed her foot into the pump and started to rise.

"Wait!" He reached across the table, taking her hand in a firm grip. "Your name and address?"

"What on earth would you need with that?"

"The way you leave things about, it might be convenient in case I have to return something...a bracelet or a shoe or—"

"I'm not leaving anything with you! Nor do I intend to see you ever again!"

"If you could see me," he said, chuckling, "you wouldn't be here now."

Cicely snatched her hand away and stood up. She had to escape from this man even if she went in the wrong direction. Perhaps, if she could find a waiter...

"This way, my dear." He came around the table and took her arm. "Your name?" he asked again as he led her across the room. When she remained silent, he prompted, "Surely you'd rather present me to your escort as an old acquaintance than as a casual pickup?"

"Oh! Cicely," she said hurriedly. "Cicely Roberts."

"Well, now, it's been a pleasure, Cicely Roberts. And hadn't you better smile?" His voice was low and teasing as he added, "Quite remarkable, you know, the way you manage to smile and frown at the same time."

She had no chance to answer, for they had at last reached her table.

"I'm delighted you decided to join me." Spencer spoke in the miffed tones of a man unaccustomed to being abandoned by his female companions.

"I'm afraid it's my fault," said the man who had brought her back. "I was so glad to see Cicely that I detained her to ask about her family. Please forgive me. I'm Mark Dolan." He held out a hand, which Spencer was compelled to take.

"Brick Spencer."

"So nice to meet you," he said, pulling out Cicely's chair. "Give my regards to your mother, Cicely." She caught a whiff of after-shave mingled with wine as he bent toward her. Then she felt his lips against her temple, warm and surprisingly intimate, so that for a moment there seemed to be only the two of them and she barely heard his whispered "Enjoy" before he turned and walked away.

Oh, how dare he! Cicely touched a hand to her cheek, vigorously denying to herself that she wasn't shocked by the stranger's audacity as much as she was by her own reaction to his gesture.

"He must be a very good friend, indeed." Spencer's tart voice recaptured her attention.

"No. Just a very pushy one." She spoke sharply, her anger again aroused by the other man's intrusion. That it was her own fault was momentarily forgotten. She remembered only that the man had cut into the brief precious time she had to persuade Spencer to back her proposed dress shop. And George had gone to so much trouble to arrange this meeting with his boss.

"Spencer will invest in anything that's likely to bring a profit," George had told her. Cicely felt confident that a small select dress shop in the Roseville Mall would be profitable. But she hadn't been able to convince either the bank or the Small Business Administration of this. Not without capital of her own to reinforce her optimism.

And that was stupid! Why would you want to borrow money if you already had it? The small sum salvaged from her father's life insurance had been used to supplement what Cicely earned doing alterations for The Boutique. Now that the insurance money was all gone, she was frightened. They could barely survive on her meager income, and if her mother had another attack . . .

"Coffee, Miss Roberts? Dessert?"

"Just coffee, please. No wait!" She looked up at the waiter, who was pouring her coffee. "Perhaps cheesecake, if you have any." She didn't like cheesecake, but it was something she could linger over, a way of prolonging the interview. She had not yet found the nerve or the opportunity to bring up the dress shop.

"Don't just hit him with your business proposal," George had warned. "For once in your life, try to be a little charming. Act like Alicia."

That was difficult. Cicely had always known she could never be as beautiful or as charming as her mother. And she was already in awe of Spencer, the wealthy entrepreneur George so often bragged about. At thirty-five, Spencer was a financial wizard who, according to George, had a reputation for spotting a tottering business and moving in to make or break it. How could she interest such a man in a small retail dress shop? But this was a matter of survival for her, so she had to try.

"I've heard so much about you," she'd murmured earlier in the evening when George introduced her. She'd tried to smile as Alicia would have, tried to make her eyes beguiling. And then she'd been thrown completely off guard by Spencer's first words.

"George, where have you been hiding this beautiful lady?" He had spoken in a tone of such obvious admiration that Cicely flushed. "It was kind of you to join me for dinner, Miss Roberts. This makes my California trip worthwhile." After seating her, he turned to George. "Ah, yes, you do have that contract business to look after, don't you?"

"I'm on my way," George answered. "Cissy, I'll return for you at eleven. Enjoy your dinner." Then, to Cicely's consternation, he had taken his leave, *with her glasses in his pocket*.

"Now, my dear," Spencer had said, as he sat down across from her, "We must get better acquainted. Tell me about yourself."

"There really isn't much to tell," Cicely stammered. "I'm a seamstress, and—"

"A seamstress!" He laughed. "Now, that's unusual. I don't believe I've ever met a seamstress before. And I must say you don't meet my conception of one. Not with those classic features. If you'd said you were in television or modeling, I wouldn't have been surprised."

All through dinner, he'd peppered his conversation with such flattering comments that Cicely felt herself at a loss. She could have basked in his admiration had she been able to believe it. Or, had she known how, she might have used it to further her own interests. But this kind of attention was so unexpected and so unlike anything she'd ever experienced, that Cicely hardly knew how to respond. At least she remembered to "act like Alicia" and interest herself in the affairs of her companion.

"George said you were pleased with the results of the hearing this morning. I'm glad," she said, trying to recall what it was about. Offshore oil leases?

"Yes, but it went pretty much as I expected." He sounded so assured, so confident.

"Then you weren't surprised?"

"My dear, there's no room in this business for surprises. The first step is to survey the whole, to foresee the unforeseeable."

"Oh?"

"Yes, indeed. For example...I was approached by the owners of a flour mill in Topeka...." Spencer launched into a series of examples that quite overwhelmed Cicely. She felt a little dizzy as she heard him switch from the flour mill to a coffee plantation in Kenya and then to a floundering British airline. She marveled at his deft handling of each venture, the way he could discern immediately what was wrong and how many thousands or millions would be needed to set it right. She was keenly aware of this man's power—and of her own insecurity and insignificance. All evening, she'd been too intimidated to even mention the little dress shop.

But this is it, she thought as the waiter poured her coffee. Her only opportunity. If she didn't ask him now...

"Mr. Spencer," she said timidly, when the waiter had departed, "I'd like to ask your advice about something." This was underhanded. Asking for advice when what she really wanted was money.

"Certainly, my dear."

"I've been thinking of...well, I live in Roseville, about forty-five minutes from Sacramento. It's a residential community." She hesitated, taking a sip of coffee, then plunged into her appeal. "It's really an excellent location for an exclusive dress shop." She referred to the nearby military bases and newly developed industries. She spoke of the growing number of career women and executives' wives who lived there and were forced to go to Sacramento or San Francisco for their major shopping. Her enthusiasm grew, and she forgot her awe of Spencer, forgot to "be Alicia." She was Cicely, characteristically blunt and direct, as her ideas spilled out of her.

"Well now, Miss Roberts," Spencer said slowly when she paused for breath, "I can see you've given this project a great deal of thought."

"Yes." She leaned toward him, wishing she could see his face. His tone had been noncommittal, and she couldn't tell whether he was bored, excited or indifferent.

"You've asked for my advice, and quite frankly—" He broke off as the waiter set their desserts before them and refilled their coffee cups. Then he continued. "Let's think about this. A small shop. As I said before, when anticipating any proposed venture, one must first survey the whole situation."

"Yes." Cicely gripped her dessert fork and took a deep breath.

"If you looked at the existing surveys, you'd find that such shops have a history of eighty percent failure. This cheesecake is delicious. Good choice. But you haven't tasted yours."

"Oh!" Cicely lifted a small sliver to her mouth. It felt like a tasteless gluey mass, but she managed to swallow it. "So you think it's not such a good idea?"

"Well, for one thing, there's no way that small retail establishments can compete with the volume and prices of large department stores."

"I see," she said, quite daunted. This had not occurred to her.

"And take a look at your potential customers." There was a slight pause, and she heard the clink of his cup against the saucer. "Women stuck in a small community... Roseville, did you say?"

She nodded.

"I think such women would find a shopping spree to a nearby city a pleasant excursion rather than an inconvenience. Probably more convenient, in fact, affording them a choice of department stores where they already possess credit cards. No, my dear—" she could tell he was shaking his head "—I think you would find such a venture unprofitable."

"But if the shop had special items?"

"Such as?"

"I had planned to feature exclusive designer dresses."

"How would you manage that?"

"Well, I design clothes and sometimes—"

"Oh, do you now!" he remarked, as if glad to change the subject. "Tell me, when does a beautiful girl like you find the time for a hobby?"

. "Well, I do," Cicely said. "You see, I like designing and—"

"And one always has time for what one likes, eh? Tell me, pretty lady, what else do you enjoy?"

"Well, I..." Cicely stammered. *Beautiful girl. Pretty lady.* She didn't feel beautiful. She was miserable. She couldn't see, her feet hurt and he was resorting to small talk. He wouldn't finance the shop. Worse than that—this was a man who knew what he was talking about, and his doubts had destroyed her own confidence in the possibilities of her plan, even if she managed to find the money.

It was as if the props had been knocked out from under her. What could she do? The only thing she really did well was sew, and—

"How often are you in New York, Miss Roberts...Cicely?"

"New York? Why, I've never even been there."

"Well now, that's a shame! You must come. Really. I'm sorry my time here is so short, but I'd like to see more of you. Perhaps we can arrange a trip. I'd love to show you New York—and I'd like to show *you* to New York. Listen, there are some great shows opening on Broadway now and—oh, here's George. George, I've been telling this young lady she ought to come to New York."

Cicely was relieved to see George. She wanted to snatch her glasses from his pocket, kick off her shoes and get out. But George sat down and ordered coffee, so she was obliged to smile and engage in another half hour of small talk before she could escape.

"Thank you for dinner, Mr. Spencer," she said politely when they were finally leaving. "It's been a delightful evening."

"Indeed it has. And it will certainly not be the last dinner we share. George, you must persuade this charming young lady to come to New York for a visit. Do you know she's never been there? We'll have to show her the town."

MARK DOLAN SIPPED his coffee and watched Cicely walk out with the two men. As a matter of fact, he'd been watching her ever since she left his table. Even from across the room he could tell how much in awe she was of her companion. How she looked at him with deference and hung on his every word.

And the guy was eating it up!

Let's face it, Dolan, if she looked at you like that, you'd feel pretty smug, too. He grinned, admitting the truth of this. When she'd joined him, he thought... Well, never mind what he'd thought. The minute he had looked into those eyes, he'd known this was a woman completely without guile, as artless as a child. But, he remembered with a chuckle, she had the temperament of a woman. "I didn't ask for a lecture. I just want directions."

He studied the man across from her. Self-assured and assertive, he bore all the marks of success. Just the type an insecure girl like that would fall for.

He pondered the thought. Insecure. Yes, that was the word. So insecure that she'd left her glasses off even though she couldn't see beyond her nose without them! And what did she hope to accomplish by this charade? Didn't she know there were other qualities more important, more meaningful than a flawless physical appearance? Besides, she couldn't leave her glasses off forever. Silly, insecure, vain. Not his type, thank goodness.

Still, there was something about those eyes, that determined tilt of her chin.... Cicely. Cicely Roberts. Would she be in the phone book?

CHAPTER TWO

AS SOON AS SHE GOT into the car, Cicely took off her shoes and reached into George's pocket to retrieve her glasses.

"I'll never leave these off again!" she vowed, as she slipped them on. Cars, buildings and the lights and shadows of the night came suddenly into focus. The glasses with their sturdy frames and extra-thick lenses weighed heavily on her small nose. But cumbersome and awkward though they were, Cicely remembered how helpless she'd been without them. Sightless. Completely at the mercy of that obnoxious man!

She must have muttered aloud, because George shot her a quick surprised glance. "Who? Spencer?" he asked incredulously, as he maneuvered the car onto the freeway.

"No. A man I ... bumped into. And whom I hope never to see again!" She bit her lip, reminded of the stranger's words. *If you* could *see me...* "No," she said hastily. "Not Spencer."

"I didn't think you were talking about Spencer. I could tell he was quite smitten with you, Cissy."

"Well, it doesn't matter," she sighed. Her hopes for the dress shop had been thoroughly dashed.

"Sure, it matters. He wouldn't have given you the time of day, the way you looked this morning." George's chubby frame shook as he gave a deep-throated laugh. "You came into that hotel looking like Cinderella before she met her fairy godmother."

"And I suppose you think you're the fairy godmother!"

"Darn tootin'. You have to admit Alicia and I pulled the fastest transformation in history."

"And all for nothing." Everything George and her mother had put her through—hair, makeup, squeezing her into those shoes and taking off her glasses—had been for nothing. She touched the soft fabric of her dress. One of her best creations. Now she'd have to have it cleaned before she could take it to The Boutique, which would receive fifty percent of whatever it brought, never mind the cost of the material and the time and labor. If she had her own shop...

"What do you mean, all for nothing? Spencer didn't go for the dress shop? He won't back you?"

She shook her head.

"Gosh, Cissy, I'm sorry. I wanted to help."

"You did help. If I hadn't talked to Spencer, I'd still be chasing a rainbow. Knocking myself out, trying to start a project he tells me would almost certainly fail."

She thought of Spencer, his quick business acumen, how decisively he'd pointed out problems that had never occurred to her. "I'm glad I had a chance to talk with him. Thank you, George," she said fondly, touching his arm.

George was her very best friend, like an older brother. He was the boy next door who had fought the boys who called her "goggle-eyes." He had taken her to the high school dances when no one else would. He'd finished college the same year she finished high school, and that summer he had married Joanne and moved to New York. But they'd kept in touch, and two months ago, when he had returned to finalize the sale of his parents' home, she'd told him about her plans and loan problems. She had been so excited when he'd phoned last week to say that he and his boss would be in Sacramento on Tuesday, and perhaps Spencer might be interested in investing in the shop.

"I know you're disappointed," George said. "I'm sorry."

"Don't say that! You saved me from pursuing a disastrous project. I'll come up with a better one," she said brightly, not wanting even George to know how desperate her situation had become. She quickly changed the subject, asking him about Stella, his mother. "How does she like the big city?"

"Much better since she has a new grandbaby to care for."

"I really miss her," Cicely said, thinking of the many happy hours spent playing beside Stella's old sewing machine while her parents were away at parties or on trips. "It was Stella who taught me to sew."

"Like I miss your dad," George answered. "He was the only one who came to my Little League games." And so they talked of earlier years until they reached Cicely's big old-fashioned house.

"Give Stella and Joanne my love, and kiss the baby for me," she said, as she opened her door. "You have a good trip back. And thanks again, George. It does help to know what not to do."

Once inside, she locked the door and for a moment leaned against it, her head pounding. She felt bone-tired, defeated and anxious. She took a deep breath, then resolutely lifted her shoulders and, still in her stocking feet, went up the wide staircase, moving quietly so she wouldn't disturb her mother. Alicia was always in and asleep long before this. But when she reached the landing and saw the light under the door, she felt an immediate jolt of fear. Was something wrong? Her exhaustion forgotten, Cicely hurried into the bedroom, hoping her mother had not had another asthma attack.

She was relieved to find Alicia lying relaxed against a pile of pillows, eyes closed, two slender fingers caught between the pages of the book on her lap. She looked so serene that Cicely hated to disturb her. Even under the intense glare of the bedside lamp, the small oval face with the perfect patrician features looked young, the pale translucent skin smooth and unlined. The few streaks of silver in her hair only highlighted the gold, belying her forty-nine years. The hair was tied with a ribbon that matched the blue of her bed jacket. Alicia always remembered these little touches, and Cicely smiled indulgently as she gently started to remove the book.

"Oh, Cissy, you're home!" The long lashes fluttered open and Alicia spoke in a rush. "I'm so glad you're back. I get so nervous alone in the house. I haven't been able to sleep a wink!"

"I'm so sorry." Cicely took the book and laid it face-down on the table. "But I'm here now, and I'll bring you a mug of warm milk. That always makes you sleep."

"That would be so nice, dear. I haven't eaten a thing since lunch."

"Alicia!" Cicely, in the process of hanging up her mother's mink jacket, turned toward her. "I left chicken in the oven, and salad in the fridge and—"

"I know. But I didn't seem hungry. And you know how I hate to eat alone."

"Well, we'll take care of that right now," Cicely said cheerfully. "Just let me get out of this dress." In her own room, she changed into a robe, then went back downstairs.

"Oh, sweetheart, you're so good to me," Alicia said, when Cicely returned with the tray. "Now sit here and tell me all about your evening. It was sweet of George to arrange for you to meet his boss. Is he nice?" she asked, as she took a sip of hot chocolate and broke off a piece of buttered toast.

"Yes. Very nice."

"And where did you go? Did you have a good time?"

"Yes," Cicely answered, forbearing to mention that the purpose had not been to have a good time. It upset Alicia to talk about money problems. So Cicely told her where they'd gone, what they had eaten, and yes, Mr. Spencer was a very interesting, very handsome man.

"Oh, I'm so glad you had a good time," her mother said, as she daintily put the tray aside. "And you looked so pretty, Cissy. I couldn't believe it was you. I'm glad George made you take off those horrible glasses. It's such a pity you can't wear contacts."

"Oh, Alicia. Please. We tried that!" Even now Cicely could remember the painful burning, and how red and swollen her eyes had become. She would never be able to wear contacts, the doctor had said, because she was allergic to them.

"I know." Alicia sighed. "But those glasses just swallow up your face. They're so big and clumsy."

"Oh, well," Cicely replied with a short laugh. "They may not be much to look *at*, but they're sure useful for looking *through*." And for fending off obnoxious men who thought not seeing was funny! Poor Alicia, she thought, as she put away the black pumps and caught a glimpse of all the beautiful things her mother wore so seldom now. No more parties or trips. The only social affair in which she still participated was the couples' bridge club, which continued to meet at her house every Thursday evening. Alicia enjoyed so few pleasures now—not even vicariously through me, Cicely thought.

After she smoothed the pillows and settled her mother in bed, she turned out the lamp and took the tray downstairs. Cicely worried about Alicia, and longed for the lovely vibrant woman she'd been before her husband's death, two years before. Cecil Roberts's sudden death at fifty-two was a shock for both women. Cicely had been summoned home from design school for the funeral. Almost before it was over, Alicia had to be hospitalized with the first of the terrible recurring asthma attacks.

"The shock has been too much for her," the doctor said. "She can't tolerate another upset."

So it was Cicely to whom the lawyer explained the state of their financial affairs. And it was Cicely who shouldered the responsibility, determined to keep a roof over their heads and to look after her mother. The asthma attacks continued and sapped Alicia's strength, and despite the passage of time, she had not ceased to mourn the husband she had lost.

"She married him when she was eighteen," Stella had once told Cicely. "And he absolutely indulged and adored her. Their married life was one long honeymoon. She didn't have you until almost ten years later," Stella added, laughing. "I don't think she ever knew what to do with you."

Of course she didn't, Cicely had thought then. Instead of a replica of her own delicate blond beauty, Alicia was saddled with her—an ugly-duckling daughter with her father's unruly black hair and his tall lanky frame! Actually, Cicely was only five foot seven. But she'd grown rapidly and at twelve, had dwarfed her five-foot-two-inch mother.

Like her father, Cicely, too, adored her mother. Her happiest childhood memories were of the times she sat enveloped in a fragrant mist of powder and perfume, watching Alicia try on one dress after another. Cicely was often allowed to choose which one suited the particular occasion, before being sent off to stay with Stella, who seemed more like a mother to her than the exquisite goddess she had been trained to call "Alicia."

Strangely, Cicely never played dress-up in any of Alicia's discarded garments. Nor, as other little girls might have, did she parade around in Alicia's fancy slippers. Much of her playtime was spent lying on the floor, laboriously drawing pictures of women who looked like her mother and wore unusual costumes created in Cicely's own mind. Her father encouraged it, saying she had a flair for artistic creativity.

He should have sent me to business school instead, Cicely thought now. Office skills were more practical. But, as she had since learned, Cecil Roberts was not a practical man. If he had been, he wouldn't have allowed the law practice that his father had founded to deteriorate so rapidly. In Cecil's hands, old clients had disappeared and few new ones had been added. Cicely realized now that he had neglected the business and spent his time pursuing the hobbies he loved—his wood carving and tennis. Though the business dwindled, he and Alicia had never curtailed the extravagant manner in which they lived. They took trips, gave fabulous parties and sent Cicely to the best schools. Until her father's death, there had been no indication of the sad state of his financial affairs.

Cicely shook her head. How could a lawyer have mismanaged so badly? From the windowsill above the sink, she took down the wooden figure of a swan and ran a finger along the smooth graceful lines. She remembered her father sitting on the back lawn, happily whittling away at a wood carving. He had loved working with his hands. It was clear to her now that he was never meant to be a lawyer. He had bent to the pressures of his own father's expectations, obedient but too undisciplined to succeed. And perhaps too dependent on his father, too sure that what had always been provided would always be available.

Cicely drew a deep breath. She had loved her laughing, carefree father and had taken all he gave without question. Now she regretted that she'd never understood his turmoil, never realized how he had schemed, borrowing on his insurance and refinancing the home he had inherited. And he'd done it all for Alicia and for her—to give them everything they wanted and certainly more than they needed. As she replaced the little swan, she marveled at how well her father had insulated them. Protected them. Sheltered them from the harsh realities he had faced then, and she must face now.

She put the mug and plate in the dishwasher and went wearily upstairs, wondering what she could do. She was finding it difficult to keep up the mortgage payments; she'd thought of selling the house, but they had to live somewhere. Besides, what would she do without the attic? Her father had finished it for her, lining one wall with big windows, installing a stereo and smooth hardwood floors so she and her friends could dance. But Cicely had been a rather shy teenager, and the room had rarely been used for its intended purpose. However, it now made an excellent workshop, and she didn't see how she could manage without it.

Tomorrow was the first of the month. Cicely climbed into bed, mentally balancing the mortgage payment and other monthly bills against the check she would get from The Boutique. Her head ached, and the figures became muddled, and she soon fell into a restless sleep, a sleep punctuated by vague dreams of a tall stranger.

CICELY. CICELY ROBERTS. He couldn't get her out of his mind.

Mark Dolan stopped writing and tapped his pencil against the desk. Finally he put down the pencil, leaned back in the big leather chair and watched the February rain splatter against the windows of the den.

It was at home in England on just such a day that he had started the book. He had tramped through the woods as he often did, slushing through the wet leaves, feeling the rain on his face, thinking. Mostly he thought about his patients, and the fact that he was tired. Tired of listening to people complain how they, or more often someone else, had messed up their lives. He was tired of trying to lead them out of the traps they'd fashioned for themselves. He listened and tried to stifle the inner voice that cried, *They're too late.*

If only he could tell people how to avoid the emotional traps, give them some kind of direction, write a guidebook on how to be happy. He kept thinking about it as he walked back to the manor house.

It had been a whim, really. But he'd put his thoughts on paper and had the whole thing typed up. Then he'd given it to an agent he knew. No one had been more surprised than he when the agent brought him a healthy contract from an American publishing company. He was surprised, but inspired; he quickly completed the outline and set up a writing schedule. But he made little progress.

He couldn't seem to find the time or the place to write. The country estate, which had been in his family for generations, was less than a hundred miles from London and should have been ideal. But there were tourists—necessary because the taxes had to be paid and the place maintained, even if no one lived there. He and his older sister, Lisa, were the present owners. Lisa lived with her husband and children in California, and Mark had his flat in London. Actually, he could have gone down to the country and hidden himself away in some isolated part of the manor house, or in the back room of Timothy's lodge. But he was inevitably drawn to and distracted by the tourists. An old man would rub a hand lovingly over the wood of the banister Mark had often slid down as a child. And Mark would wonder what made the old man love the wood, and what had put the sadness in his face. He would wonder about the laughter in one woman's eyes, and the tight pinched lines about the eyes of another. Lisa said he was a people watcher.

Of course, it was impossible to write in London, what with his patients, his friends and his clubs. And women.

"Women will always be a problem for you, dear brother," Lisa explained on one of her home visits, when they walked together in the woods. "It's your dreamy hazel eyes, and that sexy cleft in your chin," she said, laughing.

"And when you stare at a lady in that quizzical way of yours and begin to ask gentle teasing questions, she thinks it's a come-on. She thinks you're utterly fascinated with her. What she doesn't understand is that you're simply examining her—as you would a worm under a microscope!"

He protested at that, saying he never thought of women as worms. He liked women.

"That's just it. You like *all* of them. But you're over thirty now, and I wonder when one of them will really capture your heart. Meanwhile," she said, tucking her arm in his, "I suggest that you remove yourself from your present feminine entanglements, and come back to America with me. It's an ideal arrangement. You can live in our guest house and do your writing. You can tramp around in the woods and do your thinking. And I promise to keep the boys out of your hair."

He had not gone back with her then. But two months later, he turned his patients over to his partner and followed her. Lisa had been true to her word, and the family had not intruded on his privacy. He had stuck to his schedule, avoided entanglements, and the work had progressed rapidly. He was now completing his final draft, and if he kept to his routine...

Rising abruptly, he walked over to the window, then stood there staring out. The rain had almost stopped, and he watched a squirrel run across the yard and up the trunk of a tree.

There had been something in that girl's eyes. Something scared—but something brave and determined, too.

Cicely. Cicely Roberts. She must be in the phone book.

CICELY LOVED the rain. Whenever it splashed against the windows and drummed on the roof, she felt warm and secure in her attic workshop. Capable. As if she could whip up a dozen heavenly creations and sell them for a fantastic sum that would pay off the mortgage. She chuckled. Well, she had one dress finished, anyway. And if she cut out the jumpsuit tonight and finished it tomorrow... Perhaps two outfits would bring in *one* mortgage payment.

She glanced at her watch; it was time to set up for her mother's bridge session. She put away the scissors and took the pincushion from her wrist, then bounded downstairs to arrange the tables and chairs.

"Do you think we should have a fire?" Alicia asked, as she distributed the cards and tallies. "It always makes the room so cheerful."

"I think that would be nice," Cicely agreed. She got an armful of logs from the patio and started the fire while Alicia filled the coffee urn and set out refreshments. Then Alicia hurried upstairs to change and Cicely, noticing that the rain had stopped, went outside to pick some flowers for the buffet.

The camellia bushes at the corner of the house were large and sturdy, so she wasn't surprised to find that many of the rich red blossoms had survived the rain. She was at the kitchen sink, shaking the water off the leaves, when the phone rang. She lifted the receiver, praying it wasn't a cancellation for bridge, in which case she'd have to fill in.

"Hello," she said.

"Cicely? Cicely Roberts?"

"Yes?"

"It's Mark Dolan."

"I beg your pardon?" she asked, trying to place the name.

"We met on Tuesday evening when you...er...graced my table."

"Oh. Oh, yes." There was a catch in her throat as she recognized the husky British accent.

"I wonder if you'd have dinner with me. Tomorrow night, or if another time is more convenient..."

"I . . . well . . ." For a moment she was speechless. Men seldom—almost never—asked her out. And now this man she'd just . . . well, not even met. Not even seen, actually. He had kissed her, just a casual touch, but it had sent her senses reeling, and . . .

"Well?" he prompted.

"I . . . I don't go out on dates . . ." This was such an embarrassing truth that she hastened to add, "With men I meet on the street."

He gave a low chuckle. "But we didn't meet on the street. We met in a perfectly respectable restaurant."

"My mother would call that the street."

He laughed. The hearty laugh she remembered. She felt a tingling sensation, eager, excited. That laugh. That voice. She had a sudden desire to know what he looked like. Maybe . . . But this was ridiculous. She didn't know this man.

"No, I don't think so. Thank you very much, Mr. Davis."

"Dolan."

"What?"

"Dolan. Mark Dolan."

"Oh. Yes. Mr. Dolan. I'm sorry, but I'm very busy and—"

"Wait. Don't hang up. You left something with me."

"I'm sure I didn't. . . ." She paused, thinking. "I'm sure I didn't leave anything with you."

"Oh, yes, you did." His voice was low and sensual. "A haunting memory. A vision of a beautiful lady with such lovely blue eyes I can't seem to forget them."

Me? Was he talking about her? Then she remembered. He hadn't seen *her*, either. He had seen her Cinderella garb, discarded as quickly as she'd removed her mother's shoes.

Oh, Lord! If she saw *him*, he would see *her*.

"I'm sorry, Mr. Dolan," she said with finality. "I—I can't. Thank you, but . . . I'm very busy. Please excuse me. Goodbye." She hung up quickly.

CHAPTER THREE

CICELY STARED at the phone, feeling a sudden inexplicable wave of disappointment. She would never know what he looked like, would never again hear the husky British voice with its undercurrent of teasing laughter. And she would never again, she thought, experience that easy camaraderie, that unfamiliar joy.

She picked up a sprig of camellia leaves and shook it vigorously. What on earth was she thinking of? There had been nothing joyous about that evening. She'd felt so lost, wandering around as if in a dream. And more than anything, she'd felt irritated with that... what was his name? Dolan. Mark Dolan. She'd been furious because he had delayed her from her real business.

Still, there was something in his manner, in the way he'd talked with her. Like... flirting? Not exactly flirting. But as if he, well, liked her. As if he found her interesting. And for just a moment she'd felt... accepted. As though she belonged.

All her life Cicely had felt apart. In high school, she would sit in some isolated corner of the classroom or gym and watch the others through her thick-lensed glasses. With painful self-consciousness, she would watch girls like Debby. Laughing, chatting, always the center of a happy group. Or walking arm in arm with an admiring male, casually exchanging lighthearted remarks. Debby had been homecoming queen and was almost as pretty as Alicia.

"Beauty is as beauty does," Stella often used to tell her. And Cicely had worked hard to do everything right. She had stayed on the honor roll, sung in the glee club, made all the costumes for the school plays—because at fifteen she could whip up a dress as quickly as Stella herself. But never, even in the glee club, had she really been part of the group. She always felt clumsy and awkward and never achieved a friendly camaraderie with anyone, certainly no male. Except George, of course, who was more like a big brother.

But that evening, with that man, even though she'd felt tense and anxious, there had been *something*. A kind of togetherness. An easy rapport. The way he'd taken her back to Mr. Spencer, pretending to be an old friend. The way he had kissed her. She touched her temple, feeling a burning now, as she had when his lips brushed that spot, so lightly and casually.

And he had liked her! He had looked up her number, and called, and invited her out.

And you turned him down. You could have gone out with him this very evening while Alicia's occupied with her bridge. You could have...

No, it wouldn't be the same, Cicely thought, as she adjusted her glasses. Resolutely she stuffed the last flower into the bowl, which she carried to the refreshment table. She put another log on the fire, and sternly told herself to stop mooning over a complete stranger and get back to work. She went upstairs, stopping on the second floor to check on Alicia.

"Everything's ready downstairs," she told her mother. "You look wonderful in that dress. Here, let me tie the belt. It goes this way. Now, you have a good time. And, if you need me, just buzz," she added, once again thankful for the intercom system her father had installed, making it possible for her mother to summon her from any room in the house.

She reached her attic workshop, and stood for a moment, contemplating the two parachutes she had purchased at the flea market, one a beautiful sky-blue, the other silver-gray. The purchase had made quite a dent in her budget, but they were worth it.

Parachute silk. She decided to fashion the jumpsuit from the gray, and fingered the material, loving the soft luxurious feel of it. Then she put the parachute aside and began to unroll a bolt of muslin. As usual, she would try out her design by sewing the garment from the cheap cloth first.

She worked steadily, trying to push out of her mind the strangely persistent thoughts of a man with laughter in his voice, a man she would never see, never really know.

HER PLACE SHOULDN'T BE too hard to find, Mark Dolan thought, as he took the first turnoff for the small suburb of Roseville.

The rain had returned, but off and on sharp glints of sun appeared through the mist. It gave the early-evening light an eerie effect and made the unfamiliar streets of Roseville look dusky and indistinct.

Why, he puzzled, was he pursuing Cicely Roberts? Why hadn't her emphatic "No, thank you" deterred him? *Perhaps because "no, thank you" so seldom comes your way, and you can't take it, you conceited jerk!*

He grinned to himself. No, he argued, it was because she was somehow different. And her refusal hadn't been all that emphatic. There had been a hesitancy. He chuckled. With her repeated "I'm very busy" she'd sounded as befuddled over the phone as she had appeared that evening.

So maybe it was curiosity, then. He'd like to see what such a woman was busy *at*. No. It wasn't just that. There *had* been something about her. An unexpectedly magnetic quality. Something that drew him, despite himself.

Swanson Way was a quiet street. Full of big old-fashioned houses set back on generous lawns. That surprised him. He'd expected her to live in an apartment. But no, 1905 Swanson Way was a big brick house like the surrounding ones, with a wide old-fashioned front porch. He mounted the steps and rang the doorbell.

The door was opened by an exceptionally beautiful woman, who did not seem at all surprised to see him.

"Oh, hello," she said. "You're Mr. Simmons, of course. Do come in."

"No. I'm Dolan. Mark Dolan."

"Oh, I am sorry. I was sure Rita said Simmons. But do come in out of this weather. I see it's started raining again."

Mark stepped into a large entry hall and studied the woman, who looked trim and smart in a beige knit dress. No resemblance at all, he thought. Only...yes, the eyes. He looked down at a pair of elegant taupe pumps. *It's my mother's shoe, and she wears a half size smaller.*

"Mrs. Roberts?" he ventured.

"Yes. But do call me Alicia." She smiled. "And let me take your coat. You're a bit early. But the others should be here soon." She never stopped talking as she took his raincoat and hung it in a closet. "It's sweet of you to take Rita's place. And on such short notice, too. I do hope Rita hasn't got that horrible virus that's going around. I had a bout last month and it hung on for the longest time. But you must be freezing. Come in and have a cup of hot coffee while we wait."

He had no choice but to follow her through French doors into a living room that, along with its traditional furnishings in rich tones of copper and gold, easily accommodated four card tables and chairs, obviously arranged for a card game. Bridge? A cheerful fire blazed in the stone fireplace, and refreshments were set out on a side table. He must have stumbled into a party. He had to explain and apologize.

"Listen, Mrs. Roberts, I—"

"Cream? Sugar?" she asked, lifting an exquisitely shaped silver coffeepot.

"Ah...no thanks." He didn't want coffee, either, but she gave him no chance to refuse. "Thank you," he said, as she placed a delicate cup and saucer before him. No mug. He smiled, remembering his "We didn't meet on the street. We met in a perfectly respectable restaurant," and her answer, "My mother would call that the street."

She was right. Her mother was a very proper lady indeed, and he'd better start explaining immediately who he was.

"Mrs. Roberts—"

"Now, you must call me Alicia. We're very informal, you know. And before the rest arrive, I'd better tell you about Jake. He'll be your partner, you know, because Sue plays with him. But he sometimes gets so irritated with her, especially when he bids the short club. You know the short club bid?"

"Well, yes," he answered automatically. "But—"

"Good. Because Jake is so precise about that. But you'll have his card. You know, we all have these cards explaining our bidding system. Cecil made us do that." She went on to say that Cecil, her husband, had formed the group in this very room more than ten years ago. "And we've been meeting here ever since, every Thursday night."

Mark stopped trying to explain himself. He watched with interest as she waved slim, well-manicured hands back and forth as she talked, never pausing for an instant to question who or what he was. This was a woman, he decided, completely absorbed in herself and her own affairs.

"I was deeply shattered by Cecil's death, you know. Actually, I haven't been well since then. He was such a dear man." The blue eyes became somber, and for a moment he thought she was going to cry. But she blinked rapidly and continued, "We never once gather in this room that I don't think of him. And sometimes I think I shouldn't.... But Cicely says—in fact, she insists—that I continue the bridge sessions. She says that, well, it's something that keeps me going and— Oh, my!" she exclaimed, as a log broke and sputtered in the fireplace. "Maybe..." She looked helplessly at Mark, who was already on his feet. She watched as he reached for the tongs and replaced the log. "I don't think Cicely arranged those logs at all correctly. And maybe we'd better add another."

Mark had already taken two logs from their ornate holder, and was placing them on the grate. He smiled to himself; clearly this woman was accustomed to giving commands and being waited on. He turned from the fireplace, and dusting his hands, broke forcibly into her expression of thanks.

"Mrs. Roberts, I must tell you I am not Mr. Simmons. I'm Mark Dolan, and I came to see Cicely. If I could—"

"Cicely? You came to see Cicely?" This seemed to shock her into silence, and for the first time, she registered surprise.

Didn't anyone ever come to see Cicely? he wondered.

"I met her on Tuesday night, and—"

"Oh!" Understanding dawned in the wide blue eyes. "Oh, yes, of course. You're George's boss."

"George?"

"Yes, of course. She told me how handsome you were. How nice that you're back in town. Or did you leave? I thought Cicely said you were gone. But—how nice. Let me buzz her. She'll be so glad to see you." She moved toward the wall, but cast a puzzled glance back at him. "Your hair isn't red. Not at all."

Just as she started to press a switch, the doorbell rang and she turned away, hands fluttering.

"Oh, I must get that. They're starting to arrive. Listen, why don't you go on up?"

"Up?"

"Yes. She's in her workshop. This way." She beckoned as she walked quickly back into the entry hall. He followed, and she motioned toward a wide staircase. "Up those stairs and to the right, and up another staircase. She'll be..." But now she was opening the outer door. "Oh, hello, Chris. And how are you, Lionel? Isn't it messy out there tonight?"

Mark climbed the stairs. The lady might be proper, but she wasn't very protective. He reached the second floor and took a cursory glance around. There was a large copper urn filled with magnolia leaves against the wall in front of him. And doors leading, he supposed, to the bedrooms. He turned to the right, as directed, and proceeded up another set of stairs, narrow, but also carpeted. The strains of a Beethoven symphony floated softly down from above. The door at the top was open, and Mark stopped, staring in surprise at a large well-lighted room that seemed to be filled to capacity with a scattered array of books, papers and scraps and scraps of material. He noted a long wide table and a sewing machine, as well as a low round table with magazines piled on it.

At first he thought there was no one in the room. Then he saw her. She had her back to him, and she was kneeling on the hardwood floor. Her bare feet protruded from a pair of rolled-up jeans. She seemed oblivious of him, intent as she was upon her task, draping some material around a dress form and pinning it. He watched in silent fascination. She leaned back on her heels to gaze up at the form. Then she picked up a pair of scissors, and began to cut with a kind of reckless abandon—or so it seemed to him—beginning at the bottom, circling up toward the waist. A swath of the material fell away, and she kicked it aside as she stood and stepped backward to survey her handiwork.

"You weren't fooling," he said, almost to himself. "You really are busy."

Cicely whirled around in astonishment. There was no mistaking that voice! It was the same man who...

"You." Part of her mind wondered how on earth he happened to be here. The other half was mesmerized, taking in the handsome clean-cut features, sensitive deep-set hazel eyes, the curving mouth ready to burst into teasing laughter. "How did you get here?" she finally managed.

"Your mother directed me," he said easily. "She was rather...er...occupied, and instructed me to come right up."

"Oh." She was held by that voice, by the sight of a man she'd thought she would never meet again. The breath seemed to catch in her throat. Now that she was wearing her glasses and could see him clearly, she couldn't stop staring. He was the most attractive man she'd ever encountered in her life. Tall and lean, he exuded a casual ease, his athletic build not concealed by the expensively tailored dark brown suit. His hair was light, just as she'd thought—blond like Alicia's but without the silver streaks.

"What are you doing here?" she asked in a faint whisper.

"Chasing a vision." He spoke softly, and there was a glint of humor in his eyes. He smiled at her. She watched deep creases form in his cheeks, saw the full lips curve over very white teeth. "I told you. You left something with me. A haunting memory of a lovely lady I can't seem to forget."

Oh, Lord! Cicely felt her face burn as she looked down at her feet. She was painfully aware of how she looked in her old jeans and faded pullover, her hair twisted into a bun on top of her head. And, of course, her glasses! She wanted to speak, but somehow she couldn't seem to breathe properly.

"Please forgive me, Cicely. I wanted to see you again. I wanted to know more about you."

"So now you know." She sounded more abrupt than she'd intended.

He straightened, looked about, made a gesture encompassing the whole room. "This is your workshop?"

She nodded.

"May I?"

Again she nodded.

He began to circle the room, observing everything as if he'd come for a tour of inspection. Cicely, watching him, felt as if she were rooted to the spot. She wanted to order him out. She wanted to make a clever, offhand remark, the way someone like Debby would have. She wanted to put on her shoes. She wanted to run and hide. But that was impossible. *This* was her hiding place!

This was her sanctuary and he'd invaded it. He'd barged in here and—

"You drew this?" He was studying a design she'd sketched and tacked to the wall.

"Yes."

"Original, huh?"

"Yes."

"Clever." He moved along the wall, looking at her sketches, at the pictures she'd cut and pasted there, and the scraps of material pinned together. He turned to the low table, thumbed through fashion magazines. "Do you copy these designs?"

"No. Not exactly. I get ideas from them."

"I see." He moved backward and almost stumbled. He looked down, then back at her. "Is this a parachute?"

"Oh, yes. I—"

"Don't tell me you skydive?" He gave her such a shocked look that she gasped, laughter bubbling in her throat. "Oh, no." Suddenly she could hold back the laugh no longer. It made her feel more relaxed. "Unusual material, parachute silk. It's so flexible, so sturdy. Makes beautiful jackets, jumpsuits, dresses. Anything.''

His brow went up in a congratulatory gesture. "Very clever indeed." He came back to where she was standing, and fingered the muslin on the dress form. "What are you making out of this?"

"Just a pattern," she said.

"A pattern?"

"Yes. When I'm experimenting—drafting a pattern, that is—I first make the garment out of something cheaper, like this muslin. Materials like parachute silk are very precious."

"Ah, yes." He nodded. "That's extremely practical." He turned away from the form, and stood looking at a completed dress that hung from a rack attached to one wall. Her gaze followed his to what was her latest creation and, she thought, her best. Even from its padded hanger, it seemed to sway with a graceful elegance.

He stared at the dress for a long time, then turned an incredulous face to her. "You didn't. I mean, you couldn't." He glanced back at the dress, and again at her. "You made that?"

She could tell he was thunderstruck, and she felt a glow of pride. It was her finest work. It had taken days, with that exquisite lace of rich deep tan, carefully cutting and shirring the panels and fastening them to the soft nylon underskirt, so that they were tapered ever so slightly and fell just right, one over the other. Such an elegant dress deserved the long tight sleeves fastened at the wrist with tiny covered buttons. And the handful of rhinestones—now twinkling in the lamplight—that she'd scattered at random over the material.

She heard him give a low whistle. "That's really something. Fantastic!" His gaze swung back to the muslin-draped form. "So you start out with this." Again he focused on the lace dress. "And end with this. That's really something."

She couldn't help but smile. If he knew what she'd really started with—that delicate antique lace curtain she'd found in the thrift shop. It must have graced an oversize window in one of those old mansions they were tearing down. Despite its age, the fabric was miraculously well preserved and almost without snags.

"Tell me. How do you make it crinkle and flare out like that?" He gestured to demonstrate.

"Oh, the shirring? It's easy. I set the stitch and do it on the machine. It was the cutting and tapering that was hard." She shook her head, laughing. "I must have ripped up a dozen pieces of muslin."

"But you got it just right. Now, how the devil did you get the rhinestones on? Looks like you just tossed them and they stuck."

That was a funny way of putting it, and the laughter bubbled in her throat again. She moved to a small chest, reaching into a drawer for a packet of the fake jewels. It felt good to be explaining her methods and ideas to someone who was interested in them. Most people, even Lynn at The Boutique, only seemed interested in the finished product.

"See. They have these little prongs and you just fasten them on. These were so tiny I had to use tweezers."

"Incredible. Absolutely incredible." He wasn't looking at the rhinestones, though, but at her hands. He took one hand in his and held it, inspecting the short unpolished nails.

Embarrassed, she pulled away and replaced the packet. "You can see how easy it is to do. How simple..."

"No. Not simple at all. So this is the real Miss Cicely Roberts." He was watching her, and there was something in those hazel eyes, something so amused, so quizzical, a look so reminiscent of the boys who'd teased her, the boys George used to chase away. She straightened, tossed back the strand of hair that had slipped from its knot and lifted her chin defiantly.

"Why are you looking at me like that?" she demanded.

"Like what?" He stepped back, obviously surprised by her tone.

"Like...like you're judging me or something," she muttered.

"Oh?" He raised one eyebrow, and she saw his mouth lift in a provocative smile. "Would you like to know how you score?"

"I would not."

Ignoring her comment, he walked briskly to the table and picked up one of her sketching pads and a pencil. "Well, now, let's see," he said, striding back and forth in front of her tapping the pencil against his chin. All the while his eyes examined her intently. She felt intimidated and exposed; she didn't know what to expect or how to respond. So she just stood there, gazing at him uncertainly, one bare foot placed over the other.

"Miss Cicely Roberts." He scratched rapidly on the pad. Then he focused on her again, and she felt her face burn. "Tousled hair—sign of a busy woman. No time to slap on any makeup, either," he added, touching her cheek with the back of his hand, arousing in her a tingling excitement that did not abate even when he removed his hand to continue scribbling on the pad. "Shall we give you an eight for being natural?" He paused, considering. "No...naturalness is so rare a quality in these artificial times, I think perhaps it rates a ten."

Now his eyes roamed over her pullover and jeans, and he grinned. "Well, now, here we find a woman far too concerned with comfort and practicality." He shook his head. "That smacks of a lack of pretension. No aiming to please anybody. I'm afraid I can only give you a six on that, my dear."

His smile, Cicely decided, wasn't provocative, but gentle and coaxing, and she couldn't help but return it.

"Lack of pretension must be worth something," she argued, playing along with the game. "Surely it would rate at least a nine."

"Valid premise. Worthy of consideration." He frowned as if making a weighty decision. She watched the creases form on either side of his mouth, just as they did when he smiled, and some unidentifiable emotion, warm and vulnerable, stirred within her. "All right. Compromise. An eight for lack of pretension."

His gaze traveled downward, focusing on her bare feet. "You have an aversion to shoes, Miss Roberts?"

"Less confining." She tossed her head, totally relaxed now, and unashamed. "It lends a sense of freedom."

"Ah, yes. I can see that." He nodded in agreement. "It releases one to slash with reckless abandon through a piece of fabric. And emerge with something quite wonderful. A true symbol of freedom allowing for happy creativity. Yes, indeed. A ten for bare feet."

Cicely had to chuckle. But when he mentioned hands and reached for hers, she snatched the pad away from him.

"Mark Dolan," she announced, taking the pencil and pretending to write. "Fails to qualify for the following reasons. Not taking no for an answer. Uninvited entry into restricted territory. Insincerity, unfounded comments and undue flattery." She flashed a teasing smile as she threw the pad and pencil onto the table. "Sorry. No score."

"Not even for gallantry?"

"Gallantry?" She turned to him, puzzled.

"Yes. I restrained myself the night we met. I've restrained myself all evening. But I will do so no longer." He moved closer and lifted the heavy glasses from her nose. She felt his arm go around her, felt his lips brushing hers, casually, lightly. Then the kiss deepened, and she was consumed with a sensation so new and exhilarating that her whole body quivered. She stood on tiptoe, pressed closer and wound her arms around his neck. She was only dimly aware of the rain spattering against the windows, the soft tones of a symphony, and her mother's voice coming through the intercom.

"Cicely! Are you there, Cicely? Listen, that young man who's with you... George's boss. Can he play bridge? Because this Mr. Simmons Rita promised me was coming *isn't* coming, and—Cicely, do you hear me? Ask George's boss if he plays bridge."

CHAPTER FOUR

HE DIDN'T WANT to take his arms from around her. Her lips were warm and sweet beneath his, and her pliant, unresisting body melting against him sent a fierce current of desire through his veins. Yet the unexpected yielding, so innocently trusting, engendered in him a protectiveness that merged with and gentled his passion. His kiss became more a promise than a demand, but his arms tightened around her, as if he could hold her forever.

"Cicely! Cicely, are you there?" The voice crackling from the wall behind him became more insistent. "Cicely, ask George's boss if he plays bridge!"

Reluctantly he lifted his head and gazed down at wide blue eyes filled with wonder, parted lips looking bruised and numb, confirming his suspicion that she was as surprised by the ardor of her own response as he was.

"Cicely, answer me!"

Never taking his eyes from hers, Mark stepped backward and pressed the button. "Yes, Mrs. Roberts, I do play bridge. I'll be right down." Moving forward, he replaced Cicely's glasses and lightly touched his lips to hers. Then he smiled.

"Lips. Definitely a ten," he murmured, before he turned and went slowly down the stairs.

Cicely pressed two fingers against her mouth, as if to seal in the tenderness. She stood motionless, almost in a daze, reliving that moment when his arms had closed so possessively around her—the rough tweed of his jacket, the spicy smell of after-shave, the intoxicating pressure of his mouth on hers. It had stirred something within her so new and rapturous that she'd been seized with a delicious excitement that still lingered. She had stood on tiptoe, clutching him, wanting to taste to the full this strange ecstasy that swept through her. She had . . . she must have . . .

Oh, Lord! Could he tell that this was her first kiss? She felt the hot blood rush to her face as reality intruded, and thoughts she always kept well hidden came tumbling out. Twenty-two years old and she'd never been kissed. Well, not really.

She walked to the window and pressed her face against the cool pane, staring into darkness, remembering.

Sophomore year at high school . . . Ann Simpson's birthday party . . . Carl Adams. That sticky messy kiss planted firmly on her mouth. She'd neither expected nor wanted it. But the real humiliation came when Debby told her he had done it on a dare.

The incident hurt, and she had withdrawn even further into herself. She'd pretended she didn't mind that boys avoided her.

"Not them! You," George had insisted. "You're too standoffish, Cissy. Nobody can get near you!"

Now Cicely sighed. Whatever the reason, she'd never managed to get over her awkwardness, never had a real friend. Except for George . . . and Dan, that year at designer school. She and Dan would eat together in the cafeteria, really interested only in their projects, not each other. But he would walk her home, and when he left her at the Y, he'd kiss her. Just a little peck on the cheek. Not like . . . what had just happened.

She turned, leaned back against the window and closed her eyes, trying to recapture the magic of that kiss.

Her eyes flew open. This was ridiculous! She straightened, shaking her head as if to jolt herself back to reality.

She would not let herself be carried away by a gesture that probably meant no more to him than a casual handshake.

And if she was going to make up that mortgage payment, she'd better get busy. Deliberately, she fixed her gaze on the muslin she'd draped over the dress form. Perhaps a little gathering here. She moved a pin and adjusted the fabric to hang differently, trying hard to focus her entire attention upon the project.

It was no use! She could not get him out of her mind. Mark. Mark Dolan. A man she didn't even know. A man she met because of a curious circumstance at a restaurant. An arrogant, inquisitive, taking-over kind of man. Tonight he had just walked in, examining, touching, commenting.

And you fell for it, didn't you? All he had to do was express a little interest, throw in a few words of praise, and you acted like he'd just handed you the Coty medal for best design of the year!

Oh, yes, Cicely admitted, grinning. She had succumbed with a glow of pride, seeing her work through his eyes. Well, darn it, she had a right to be proud, she thought, as she glanced at the lace dress. He'd been impressed by it, she knew. He was the only person besides herself who had seen it, and she felt…well, that they'd shared something special.

Admit it, Cicely Roberts, you enjoyed his being here.

Oh, yes. Even when he stopped looking at the room and began looking at her! She walked over to the table to pick up the sketch pad and smiled. *Tousled hair—sign of a busy woman.* She hadn't minded. He'd made it fun. And then he'd taken off her glasses and… She caught her breath, her fingers tightening around the pad.

Her glasses. He hadn't even mentioned them. He had talked, looked, touched, and it was as if the glasses weren't there. She'd forgotten about them herself. For the first time in her life, she had watched a man look at her and been totally unconscious of her glasses.

"OH, THERE YOU ARE! Good." Alicia seized Mark's arm as soon as he entered the living room. "How fortunate that you play bridge. Cicely hates to stop working to fill in. Now let me make you acquainted with everyone." As she named names and pointed out people, Mark nodded and shook hands. "And, this," she said, as she introduced him, "is Mr. Simmons. No." Alicia waved her hand as if to erase the name. "Not Simmons. He's the one who couldn't come. You're George's boss. Mr. . . . ?"

"Dolan. Mark Dolan. But I'm not—"

"Yes. Mark. We're very informal. Now, here's Jake, your partner. You'll want to discuss your bidding system."

A short while later, Mark was seated at one of the tables, following the game easily and at the same time observing the other players. A very suspicious man, he decided of Jake, his partner, who held his cards close to his chest and frowned skeptically at Mark every time he bid.

Then there was the bald-headed man at the next table, who apologized profusely after every hand, as if whatever had gone wrong was all his fault. He ought to take a course in assertiveness, Mark thought, probably from this woman on my left . . . what's her name? Athelda? She slammed her card down triumphantly every time she won a trick, thumping the back of her hand viciously against the table. They did take this game seriously. Too seriously, he thought, as he watched Athelda trying to decide on her next bid. Her mouth was drawn into a tight thin line of concentration, and her long enameled nails beat a tattoo on the table.

Mark stared at her nails, and remembered Cicely's hands with their short, unpolished nails. He remembered those small capable hands wielding a pair of scissors carefully and expertly through the fabric, sticking a pin here or there. He liked the way she worked—joyously absorbed, taking pleasure in what she did. It was as if she were at play, while the people in this room were working.

And she was her own unerring critic. He could almost see her now, stepping backward to get a better view, kicking away that scrap of material with a bare foot.

There was something tantalizingly erotic about that bare foot, and—

"Your bid, Dolan!"

Mark started uneasily as Jake's irritated voice jarred him out of his reverie. He hated people who had to ask who bid what. But he sure didn't know what had gone on!

CICELY TOOK the lace dress to The Boutique the next day. She would have preferred to bring both outfits at once but the jumpsuit wouldn't be finished for several days, and she needed the money now. She hoped Lynn would ask a good price for the dress and, even more important, that it would sell immediately.

Lynn was ecstatic, exclaiming over and over again that it was stunning, exquisite. She tucked a six-hundred-dollar price tag in the sleeve, declaring the dress was worth every penny, if not more.

Cicely gasped. Six hundred dollars! To think that it had cost her practically nothing. Well, except for the rhinestones and the cleaning at the specialty shop where she had all her fine things done. Her share—three hundred dollars—would cover the late mortgage payment.

"Do you think it'll sell soon?" she asked. "And at that price?"

"I just don't know," Lynn admitted. "The thing is, we're between seasons just now. And most of my customers wouldn't pay that much, even for a special-occasion dress. Those who would... Size eight. Could you make it in a ten?"

"Oh, no," Cicely said quickly. "At least not in the same material." She didn't know if that kind of fine lace was available anywhere. And if it was, she couldn't afford it.

"Well, I'll say this for you, Cicely," Lynn told her with a laugh. "All your things are certainly exclusive. And believe me, this dress is worth the price. I won't sell it for a penny less."

Cicely left The Boutique, her short-lived elation displaced by apprehension. She was glad Lynn liked the dress, glad she was asking such a good price for it. But suppose it didn't sell at all!

Only two hundred dollars of the insurance money remained in the savings account. She was trying to hold on to that in case of an emergency. But the mortgage payment was overdue.... No matter what happened, she had to keep the house. Not so much for herself as for Alicia. The loss of her husband, coupled with the agonizing asthma attacks that could come upon her so suddenly, had made such an impact on Alicia that she was reluctant to leave the house. Afraid to be away from her bed and her breathing machine. But there was something else, something more significant, that only Cicely recognized. The one time her mother seemed to forget her illness was when she acted as hostess, the way she had when her husband was alive. She became her old self, a charming and gracious Alicia, every time she opened the door of the house and welcomed her friends into its large, inviting rooms. That was why Cicely had determined to keep the house and especially, to see that the Thursday night bridge sessions continued.

"Every Thursday night it's as though Cecil is still with me," her mother had once said, "and I know everything is all right because I'm leaning on him."

Still leaning on him. He'd always indulged Alicia, given her everything. And she'd thought Cecil as strong, as steady, as the rock of Gibraltar.

Cicely had reached the car now, and she sat for a moment, staring into space, the line of an Edna St. Vincent Millay poem floating through her mind. "Safe upon the solid rock the ugly houses stand: Come and see my shining palace built upon the sand!'' Even now, Alicia did not know that her shining palace had been built upon slippery grains of sand.

And I'm trying to preserve the illusion, Cicely thought. And being just as impractical as Dad, with grandiose visions of my own dress shop. No, not altogether impractical, she argued. She'd sent out at least half-a-dozen job applications; she hadn't once stopped making and trying to sell her dresses. But nothing was coming through. No dress shop, no job, no guarantee that the dress she'd worked on so hard would even sell. She pressed a hand to her forehead, feeling suddenly very tired. She was losing control, everything slipping through her fingers. Like grains of sand. If they lost the house . . .

She sat up with a show of defiance, and thrust the key into the ignition. They would not lose the house! The lace dress would sell. Hadn't every item she brought into Lynn's shop sold? And she could finish the jumpsuit in two days. She had another idea. A coatdress, double-breasted, with a wide belt of the same material. It would be stunning in that parachute silk.

She drove home rapidly, tracing the design in her mind, her fingers itching for her sketch pad. When she walked into the house, the phone was ringing. She dashed toward it, feeling a rush of excited anticipation. It could be him.

"Hello," she almost whispered.

"This is Karen Smith, from the personnel office at K. Groves. Could I speak to Cicely Roberts, please?"

"This is she." Now a more practical anticipation swept through Cicely. An interview for a job in the alterations department? Yes. Yes indeed, she could make it this afternoon. She turned from the phone, her mind filling with activity. First, Alicia's lunch. Then . . .

As she opened the refrigerator door, one of the little magnets, along with the card it was holding, fell to the floor. She picked them up, noticing that it was Dr. Davison's business card, and remembered something she'd almost forgotten. Something important. Dr. Davison had said that even though Alicia hadn't reached the required age, she was eligible for part of Cecil's social security pension because of her illness. Cicely had mailed in the doctor's form several weeks before, but they'd heard nothing yet. Since she was going to be in Sacramento this afternoon, she would stop by and inquire. If she hurried, she would have time before the three o'clock appointment at Groves. She quickly heated some soup and grilled two cheese sandwiches. Promising Alicia she'd return by six, Cicely rushed out with her sandwich in her hand.

She had to take a number and wait in line for an hour at the social security office, but it was worth it. The clerk informed her that Alicia's case had been reviewed, and she should start receiving a monthly check on April 1. A small amount, but it would certainly help.

The interview at Groves was successful, too. She'd be working in Alterations four days a week, from ten to six. Cicely left the personnel office, almost giddy with relief. They were going to make it! The regular salary, added to her mother's check, would cover the main bills, she thought, almost dancing down the escalator. Extras, and maybe even savings, would come from her Boutique earnings. Vaguely, she wondered if she could place some of her own designs at K. Groves. That is, if she still had time to design anything. Probably not, she reflected, unlocking the car. She'd be too busy taking in the bustline and making room in the hip for a customer who often had no business in the dress she was buying.

Count your blessings, Cicely Roberts, she warned herself, as she drove out of the parking lot. *A regular salary.*

You can eat and pay the rent. No more hit or miss, maybe-it-will-sell-and-maybe-it-won't!

Yet she loved designing. Sometimes she felt as if she would burst with all the ideas that came to her, inspired by the feel of a certain material or the sight of an unusual color combination. Like the crimson and purple petals of the fuchsia that hung every summer from the baskets on the patio. Perhaps she could find the time if she were well organized. She reviewed her schedule as she drove along the freeway. Monday, Tuesday, Wednesday and Friday at Groves. The ten o'clock starting time would allow her to make breakfast for herself and Alicia, and she could always fix the next day's dinner at night. Saturday she always spent at The Boutique. She had arranged to keep Thursday free, for doing the week's grocery shopping, straightening up the house and preparing for the bridge group. She felt apprehensive about leaving Alicia alone so much. But Dr. Davison had told her that as long as Alicia didn't get too excited or exert herself too much, she wasn't likely to have another attack. Cicely decided to stop by the library and pick up some more novels for her. She drove on, the busy plans echoing in her head like so many voices.

She tried to ignore a new voice that, for the first time, spoke deep inside her, sometimes surfacing with an electrifying intensity. *He likes you...he came to see you...kissed you.* A voice that urged, *It's all right! Let him into your life!* A compelling voice, bringing to mind every line of his face. She wanted to touch the crease that deepened in his cheek every time he smiled. When he called again— *If* he called... But the voice was so unfamiliar to her that she tried to stifle it.

Anyway, she told herself, he probably wouldn't call.

MARK CALLED several times during the next two weeks. But Cicely was never at home. He didn't like to ask where she was, and Alicia never volunteered the information. Somehow she always managed to divert the conversation.

"Oh, it's you, Mr. Dolan. Mark. I'm so glad you called. Did you have time to read the bridge column in today's *Bee*?"

"No. I'm afraid—"

"You should look at it. A most unusual distribution. North has six spades, jack high. South has..." An accurate account of which cards were held by each player would follow, as well as the bids and play.

He took to checking the bridge column before he called in order to forestall this discussion.

"Yes, I read it. Very good bidding," he would say. "Is Cicely—?"

"No. I disagree. You see, it only turned out that way because East led a club. Now suppose she led a heart."

"Yes, perhaps so. Do you think Cicely might—?"

"Put yourself in East's place. What do you think you would have led?"

"Oh. You're right. Possibly a heart. Listen, would you have Cicely return my call?" He gave her his number, but she was still chattering about the bridge hand and he wasn't sure she'd written it down. He hung up, wondering if she would remember that the call had been for Cicely.

Later, he began to wonder if Cicely was deliberately avoiding him. And he wondered why, as he stared at the manuscript pages spread out on his desk. He should have been writing, but he felt restless.

He stood, yawned, stretched, stared at the rosebush outside his window. New green leaves reached toward the sun; tiny buds held the promise of coming beauty. February had slipped abruptly into March, and the smell of spring was in the air. Almost without thinking, he found himself muttering Tennyson's famous words: "In the spring a young man's fancy lightly turns to thoughts of love."

Love? Dr. Mark Dolan had endured every aspect of love through his patients. He had mulled it over, been thrilled by it, agonized, even cried about it, until he was sick to death of it, and was everlastingly grateful that he was not personally involved. There had been one affair that lasted through his senior year at medical school. Very long and very painful, and he had promised himself that ...

Well, no matter! That was years ago. All of his subsequent involvements had been ... well, sometimes intimate, but always casual. Offering no promises, no commitments, no heartrending involvement.

He looked back at the phone. Why didn't she return his call? And why couldn't he get her out of his mind?

CHAPTER FIVE

"GEORGE'S BOSS called you, Cicely."

"He did?" Cicely stared at her mother. Mr. Spencer had been so definite about the dress shop. Had he changed his mind? "Did he say what he wanted?"

"No. I don't think so." Alicia fumbled with some papers near the phone. "I thought I put his number down. But maybe I didn't."

"Never mind. I'll call George." Cicely took a last swallow of coffee and kissed her mother on the cheek. "I have to run. See you tonight."

HE COULD GO over there, Mark thought. Barge right in just as he had before. But how many times could you barge in on a person who evidently didn't want to see you? Who wouldn't even return a simple phone call. Well, he'd make one more try. Early. Before Alicia had time to read the bridge column.

"Oh, Mr. Dolan, I'm so glad you called," came Alicia's cheerful voice. "I was—"

"Cicely," he cut in quickly. "Is she available?"

"Oh, I'm sorry. You just missed her. But—"

This early? She *was* avoiding him! He knew she worked at home; she couldn't be away every time he called.

"Did you tell her I called?"

"Yes. I'm sure she'll be in touch. She said she was going to call George."

"George?"

"Yes, and of course, you. But I'm glad you called because I was going to ask you..."

George first. Then me. He had thought...her response to that impromptu kiss, instantaneous and warm and... He remembered the surprise registered in those expressive eyes. He'd felt instinctively that this emotion was new to her. But maybe not. Maybe she was surprised that someone besides this George could evoke such—

"Could you, Mr. Dolan? As a favor?"

"I beg your pardon?" he asked, suddenly aware that Alicia was still talking.

"Could you take Leonard Goosby's place? His wife, Sarah, doesn't play. I can't imagine that, can you? Well, she doesn't, and she's always dragging Leonard off for some trip. So annoying! This time for a whole month. You can see where that leaves us. But you play such a good hand, and the others really enjoyed your company. We'd so much appreciate it."

Well, that was one way of barging in!

"Why, yes, Mrs. Roberts, I'll be glad to. Thank you for asking. I'll see you Thursday evening. Cheers."

He hung up the phone and picked up his pencil. George. Who on earth was George?

Well, back to work. He focused on the manuscript, began to make rapid notes. But her pixie face, framed in black hair, kept intruding.

The red-haired chap to whom he'd delivered her that first night. Arrogant, confident. Who wouldn't be, under that awestruck gaze of hers? But it hadn't been an intimate or loving look. She hadn't even been relaxed! No, that wasn't George.

There had been another chap, but he hadn't paid him much mind. George?

Well, damn! He wasn't getting anything done. Maybe a short walk would set the wheels turning. As he strode into the yard, he saw Lisa backing her station wagon out of the garage.

"Oh, good, it's you, brother dear," she called, flashing him a teasing smile. "Thinking or brooding?"

"Thinking."

"Oh, dear, I hoped you weren't—thinking or writing, I mean. Donald needs to go to the dentist.... I know I promised not to bother you," she added quickly. "But I'm really in a bind. I've got to take Denis to school, and I've got an appointment—"

"All right. Come on, tiger," he called, and eight-year-old Donald scrambled out of the station wagon.

"Thanks. And you can think while you're waiting," Lisa said lightly. Then she stopped the car to peer at him. "You look rather fierce. Are you sure you're not brooding? What's the matter?"

"Nothing. And I'm not brooding." Resentment was a destructive emotion. And he certainly bore no resentment bordering on jealousy toward a guy he didn't even know.

Mark dutifully appeared for bridge on Thursday, but didn't catch sight of Cicely the whole evening. Yet he strongly felt her presence. The artistic centerpiece of early spring flowers, the shining polish of the silver coffeepot, the arrangement of china and refreshments: these had not been wrought by magic. Nor, he decided, were they the work of Alicia's well-cared-for hands.

The next Thursday he went purposely early, and this time the door was opened by Cicely. She looked exactly as she had the last time he saw her—hair pulled up as if to get it out of her way, the same pullover, a little frayed around the collar, the rolled-up jeans. Bare feet. She looked so natural and warm, so uninhibited.

"Hello, Cicely." It came out sounding rather gruff because of a strange constriction in his throat.

"Oh. Hello." Her eyes were magnified by the thick lenses of her glasses, and he could clearly read the fleeting expression. Undisguised pleasure. Quickly replaced by...fear? Awkwardness? As if the pleasure was unaccustomed and forbidden. He felt a need to put her at ease.

"I'm so glad to find that you really do exist," he said, as he stepped inside. "I had begun to wonder."

"Oh?" Her smile was uncertain.

"You never returned my call." Her surprise was evident, and he added, "Didn't Alicia tell you I called?"

"No. That is, I don't think..." She tilted her head in a questioning gesture, and he thought, *She doesn't even remember.* But then he smelled it, too. Something burning.

"Excuse me," she murmured, and turned in a run.

He followed her through the living room and into the kitchen.

"Oh, they're ruined!" she exclaimed, as she took a sheet of cookies from the oven and placed it on the tile counter.

"No. All is not lost," he said, peering over her shoulder. "Give me a sharp knife."

They worked together, she removing the cookies with a spatula, he cutting off and discarding the burnt edges before placing them on the rack with the others. He popped one into his mouth. It was warm, crunchy and delicious.

"Very good," he said. "You can't buy these at the grocery store."

"And they cost ninety-five cents a dozen at the bakery."

"So you make them." She certainly had to go to a lot of trouble for these bridge sessions.

"Yes," she said, as if divining his thoughts. "Alicia likes everything just so."

"I see." Then why wasn't Alicia down here making everything "just so"?

Again she seemed to divine his thoughts. "My mother isn't well, and I like her to rest before her game."

"Oh?" *She looks pretty healthy to me.* "I didn't know. What's wrong?"

"She gets these terrible asthma attacks if she exerts herself too much. Tonight is her bridge night."

"I know."

"Oh, yes, that's right." She seemed rather nervous as she wiped the cookie sheet and put it away. "You played with them that other night you were here."

"Yes. And last Thursday, and again tonight if all goes well."

"Oh! I thought . . . I see. You came to play bridge."

He thought—hoped—he caught a note of disappointment.

"Well, yes. But I really came to see you."

"Oh." Her voice was muffled, and her face hidden by the door of the fridge, so there was no way to tell her reaction.

"When there was no response to my several phone calls, I became quite desperate." He seated himself on the kitchen stool and watched her emerge from the fridge with two slabs of cheese, which she began to cut into small pieces and arrange on a platter. "So when opportunity knocked, I welcomed it. Are you aware that there is a certain Mrs. Goosby who doesn't play bridge? Can you imagine that? And she's always dragging her poor husband off on some cruise or other, which, you know, leaves the bridge group at quite a loss."

His amiable mimicry of Alicia elicited a gurgle of laughter from Cicely. He liked the sound.

"So you kindly came to the rescue?" she asked.

"Not kindly. Selfishly. 'Aha,' said I, 'this is the house where Cicely lives.' So I allowed myself to be roped into the slings and arrows of outrageously serious bridge."

"Don't you like to play?"

"Let's just say that I can think of more exciting pastimes. But then, Cicely love, one should never discount any experience in life," he said, as he reached over to sample a bit of cheese. "Who would ever have thought, when my late father dragged me from my enticing youthful activities to be his bridge partner, that it would one day serve me so well? That it would be my only means of catching sight of a beautiful woman who never answers her phone, but continues to haunt me ever since she bumped into my table, took off her shoes and stumbled into my heart."

She glanced up and he caught the confused mixture of chagrin, delight and disbelief, before the eyes were quickly veiled as she gazed down at the cheese again.

"Why didn't you return my call?" he asked gently.

"I didn't know you called. You see, Alicia . . ." She hesitated, looked up, and he could see that she was once more coming to her mother's defense. "Well, we really haven't seen too much of each other lately. I've been working pretty hard."

"You should put an extension phone up there."

"Up there? Oh, you mean upstairs. No, I've been working at a real job—ten to six at K. Groves in Sacramento. You know, that exclusive clothes store, the big one. So you see I have to leave early, and I don't get back until late, and—"

"Why?"

"Well, because it takes almost an hour to get there and—"

"No. I mean, why did you take the job?" Why would anyone who could create a dress like the one he'd seen take a regular job?

"For the usual reasons. Everyone . . ." She looked at him. "Don't you have a job, Mr. Dolan?"

"Well . . ." He hesitated, remembering Lisa's "you're not only a people watcher, you're a people listener. And if people find out you're a psychiatrist, you'll never finish that book. Just say you're here for a much-needed rest or something." So he told Cicely what he had told everyone else.

"I'm on a kind of vacation. Staying with my sister...doing a little writing."

"Oh." She looked at him curiously before she picked up the platter of cheese and carried it into the living room.

"Tell me about your new job," he said, taking the cookies and following her.

"I'm doing alterations at—"

"You're doing what!"

Cicely was rather startled by the harsh note in his voice. One moment he'd been laughing and teasing, and now he was looking at her as if she'd said something scandalous.

"You're doing what?" he repeated.

"Alterations. You know, letting down hemlines and—"

"Cicely, the tables aren't up, and it's almost seven!" Alicia fluttered into the room, as pretty and dainty as a butterfly in the yellow linen dress Cicely had made for her. "Oh, dear! I do like everything ready when they arrive, and... Oh, Mr. Dolan, you're here already."

"I came early to help. Where are the tables, Mrs. Roberts?"

Cicely listened to his cheerful whistling, as he took the chairs and tables from the stairwell and set them up while Alicia directed. He was so...so comfortable, she thought with a trace of envy. Comfortable with himself—and with anyone, anywhere. That first night at the restaurant, he'd greeted her easily and talked with her as if he'd known her all his life. And tonight, he'd sat in the kitchen like...well, like George from next door. But not at all like George. That night in her workshop, he'd kissed her, a kiss that had burned on her lips and left a memory that lingered all through the week. Alicia had not told her he called. She was so forgetful, and of course they had so little time to talk. But it didn't matter now. He'd said, "I really came to see you," and she hugged the words to her heart.

"Cicely, do bring in the coffee. And do you remember what I did with the score pads?"

"Oh. I'll get them." Recalled to her duties, Cicely found the score pads and filled the coffeepot. When the guests began to arrive, she slipped quietly upstairs.

She spread a large piece of brown paper on the oversize table, and began to draw a pattern for the coatdress. From its perch in the tree outside her open window, a bird chirped lustily. A spring breeze, warm and sweet with promise, drifted in, mingling with the strange new stirring in her heart. She wondered when she'd see him again.

She saw him the very next evening.

Fridays were always hectic, and that day she worked particularly hard, missing lunch to ready three outfits for a customer who was going on a trip. When she left Alterations, she was tired and hungry. She wondered if she should get a cup of coffee before starting the long drive home.

Suddenly she was wide awake; she felt her pulse quicken, felt the sudden rapid thudding of her heart. He was there. Standing by the escalator, looking very much out of place among the throng of fashionable women, all of whom gave him more than a casual glance as they passed.

"Hello, Cicely."

"Hello." Was he there to see her?

"I was beginning to be concerned," he said glancing at his watch, "that you might have gone down on an elevator or taken another exit."

"No. I always come out this way."

"That's fortunate." He smiled as he led her onto the escalator. "I was hoping you might join me for dinner tonight."

"Oh." She'd made spaghetti the night before, and Alicia would have eaten already. But . . . Cicely was suddenly conscious of her appearance, the navy-blue corduroy skirt and plain white blouse. "No. I—I don't think so."

"You owe me, Cicely Roberts," he argued, as they passed handbags, then jewelry, and walked through the door to the outdoor shopping mall. "I suffered through three bridge sessions, waited forty-five minutes through a dozen *can I help you, sirs?* and endured the curious stares each time I shook my head, and said, 'No, thank you. I'm just waiting.' Waiting for a young lady who hasn't a 'Yes, thank you, I'd love to join you' in her whole vocabulary."

"It's just that—well, I didn't expect you." She felt a little light-headed, and there was that laugh bubbling deep inside her.

"But you *are* hungry, aren't you? We could go right across the street to the hotel where we first met, and where I so gallantly delivered you into the arms of another man."

"Well, yes. But you certainly took your time about it." She heard the laughter emerge from her throat, surprising her, and sounding, she thought, very much like one of Debby's little giggles.

They were walking toward the hotel now, as if by common consent. They could not be seated immediately, so after Cicely phoned her mother, they went into the bar to wait. It turned out to be rather a long wait, through two martinis for him, and for Cicely, two glasses of white wine.

She was unused to wine, and it usually made her sleepy. But tonight, for some reason, it made her feel vibrantly alive. She was unused to small talk, too, and at first she felt a little awkward. But as she sat in the dimly lit bar and sipped her wine, she began to relax and feel at ease with this man, who was telling her, "You interest me, Cicely. You interest me very much indeed."

"And why do I interest you?" she asked.

"I haven't decided." He sounded as if he were as puzzled about that as she. "Maybe it's because every time I see you, you're a different person."

"That's not so. George says that's what's wrong with me. He says I never make an effort to change."

"George, huh?" He frowned and stirred in his chair. "Well, I don't know about the effort, but I do perceive the changes. The last two times I saw you, you looked a barefoot abandoned waif. Tonight..." He glanced critically at her serviceable skirt and the simple white blouse, buttoned primly to her throat. "Tonight you look very much like a prissy school marm. And neither one of those images, mind you, has the slightest resemblance to the chic and stunning model I first met at this very hotel."

"Oh, but that wasn't me!" Cicely blinked as the waitress removed her empty glass and replaced it with a full one. She felt a little dizzy, and leaned toward him to explain. "George said that to impress Mr. Spencer I had to be glamorous." She giggled, feeling more and more like Debby. "I told him I was going to buy a can of that stuff."

"What stuff?" he asked, laughing.

"Glamour. Only he said it didn't come in clans...." She shook her head to clear it. "Cans, I mean. George said you have to work at it. So he and Alicia fixed me all up. And then George took my glasses. He said they spoiled the effect."

"Oh?" He was looking at her very hard. "That's what he said?"

"Yes." She nodded. "Alicia thinks so, too, you know. She always says it's such a pity." She had another sip of wine. "So when George took my glasses, she—"

"Who the devil is George?" He sounded so irked that for a moment she was taken aback.

"He—he's just a friend. He lives next door. No. That's not right. He did live next door. Now he lives in New York."

"Good." He moved the wineglass out of her reach. "I hope he stays in New York."

"Who?" She felt a little confused.

"George."

"Oh. Yes. He lives in New York, and—"

"Dolan, party of two," came the announcement over the loudspeaker. Mark came around the table and took her arm to lead her into the dining room.

"No. No wine," he told the waiter who seated them. "Could we have a little coffee first, please?" He ordered for both of them before asking Cicely, "This person you wanted to impress—was that the gentleman you were with when I first met you?"

"Yes." She took a swallow of the strong black coffee. "Spencer. Brick Spencer."

"And did you impress him?"

"No." She shook her head. "He's only interested in big things." She spread her hands wide to demonstrate. "Big shipping lines, big coffee plantations, big flour mills." Again she shook her head. "I don't know why George thought he'd be interested in a little dress shop."

"A dress shop? That's why you wanted to engage his interest?"

She nodded, watching the waiter set a bowl of steaming clam chowder before her. "But a little dress shop isn't big enough." She tasted the soup. Delicious. She hadn't realized she was so hungry. "Do you know, if you want to borrow a big amount of money, you already have to have a big amount? Don't you think it's wrong for everybody to think big?"

"Oh, sometimes it's a good idea. *You* should think big, Cicely."

"Me?"

"Yes. Why should you be working at a regular job when you can create a dress like the one you showed me the other night?"

"Possibly," she said emphatically, "because after three weeks, that dress is still hanging in The Boutique."

"That's a dress shop?"

"Yes. You see, my friend, Lynn, has this dress shop in Roseville, and I took it there. But so far it hasn't sold."

"I'm not surprised." He leaned back, thanking the waiter who removed the soup bowls.

"Why?"

"The Boutique—it sounds generic." He grinned. "Like a place where you'd buy a black and white dress with DRESS stamped across it." He paused as the waiter served their entrées. Then he picked up his knife and shook it at her. "You don't hide something like that in a place called The Boutique. That exquisite garment of yours has no more business there than you have in the alterations department of K. Groves."

"Oh? Well, I want you to know that I'm pleased, delighted and, yes, even grateful to be in the alterations department of K. Groves." She stopped putting butter on her potato to look directly at him. "It gives one a comfortable feeling, you know. A regular salary."

" 'Getting and spending, we lay waste our powers,' " he quoted, shaking his head. "There's entirely too much emphasis placed on money these days."

"Unfortunately, it's the only thing Pacific Gas and Electric will accept."

"Touché!" He laughed. "All right. I grant you that. One must work to provide the necessities of life. But you lose something when you allow the earning to become more important than the doing. Understand?"

"Not really." He wasn't making much sense, but she liked listening to his British accent. Liked his smile.

"Doing is living, Cicely." His eyes were serious and intent as he bent toward her. "Do you know how many people are unhappy because they spend their whole lives doing what they *need* to do rather than what they *want* to do?"

"Perhaps." She was glad she wasn't dizzy anymore. She needed to tell him about the facts of life. "If one has to pay the rent, one can't always—"

"Aha!" He held up his hand. "Happy is the man who can put the two together. Or in your case, love, the woman. You have an exceptional talent. A creative flair that's begging to be released. There are so many ideas twirling around in that pretty head of yours...designs so wonderful they bring a sparkle to your eyes. You want to dance around on bare feet, and sketch and paint and cut and drape and pin and create!"

She stared at him. How did he know that was the way she felt?

"There's so much joy in the doing that it doesn't feel like work. Isn't that right?"

"Well...yes. But..." She thought of her father, happily whittling away. The beautiful swan. "Sometimes that's impossible. What one wants to do doesn't always work for one."

"Unless you make it work. And don't say 'one,' Cicely. Take responsibility for yourself. A talent like yours—it's worth a try."

Suddenly she was angry. "I did try! First at the bank. And then I went to Mr. Spencer."

"You went to a man who does big things with a little idea. A dress shop. You're no salesclerk, you're a designer. Did you talk to him about that? Did you show him your sketches in that portfolio I saw on your table?"

"Well, no. Not exactly." She had mentioned special designer dresses and he'd said something about "a hobby."

"Why didn't you? If he's such a big shot, if he's launching a fleet of ships, surely he can launch a line of clothes."

"Launch a line of clothes?" she repeated, rather awestruck.

"Ah, Cicely." He shook his head. "Don't you know how special your talent is? That lace dress alone . . . superb!"

It was the most wonderful evening she'd ever spent in her whole life. She sat across the table from this handsome, dynamic man, talking with him easily and naturally. He kept telling her that she possessed an unusual talent and that she ought to make life work for her.

"I suppose I could approach Mr. Spencer again," she finally said, rather doubtfully. "But I don't like to beg."

"Beg! You're not begging. You're offering him an opportunity. A big one!"

By the time he walked her to her car, she was convinced that it was all possible.

"I think I like you best as the barefoot waif." His finger stroked her cheek and sent a tingling sensation racing through her. "You looked so happy kneeling on the floor, making magic with your pins and scissors. Promise me you'll always do what makes you happy, love."

"Yes," she whispered, ready to promise him anything.

Then he bent and kissed her. Just a light casual touch of his lips, but it set her whole being on fire. She was completely sober now, and she knew that this powerful feeling had nothing to do with the wine she'd drunk earlier. Her heart thumped so loudly that she was only dimly conscious of the garage noises and the other cars; she could not even manage an answer to his "Drive carefully."

She did drive carefully, but through a glorious haze, remembering his deep-set hazel eyes, every line of his handsome face, the way he moved and talked, exuding an air of strength and confidence. And yet he was so comfortable to be with. Comfortable and relaxed, his mouth curving as if always on the edge of laughter. She liked his hearty laugh, his crisp British accent.

Love. He had called her "love."

Oh, get a hold of yourself, Cicely. That's just one of those English expressions—like honey or babe. He probably calls every woman he meets "love." And he'll probably be returning to England soon. Going out of my life.

What's he doing here, anyway? Who *is* he?

Then it hit her like a blow. He had not said one word about himself. He had talked about her the whole evening.

No, Cicely. *You* talked about you. You babbled incessantly. You drank all that wine and...

Oh, Lord! What did I say? I must have sounded like a totally self-involved fool! Oh, Lord, what must he think of me?

WHEN HE REACHED HOME, Mark started toward the guest house, then noticed that the downstairs lights in his sister's house were on.

Good. She was still up.

He went into the living room and found Lisa curled up in the big chair, reading a novel. His brother-in-law, Richard, always the diligent eye surgeon, lay on the sofa, completely absorbed in his medical journal.

Mark greeted them both, then turned to his sister. "Listen, Lisa. There's a dress shop somewhere in Roseville, called The Boutique. And there's this lace dress...." He described it as best he could, signed a check and handed it to her. "Buy it."

"All right." Lisa looked puzzled. "For me? Do you think it'll fit or—"

"I don't care whether it fits. Or what it costs. Just buy it."

Lisa seemed at a loss for words, but Richard sat up. "A shop called The Boutique? A lace dress?" He laid aside his journal and squinted up at Mark. "Have you been drink-ing?"

"Just a couple of martinis. None of that potent wine." Mark grinned, ignoring their puzzled stares, and waved good-night.

CHAPTER SIX

IT WAS HARD for Cicely to get started the next morning. Filled with the wonder of the previous evening, she stumbled through routine duties, struggling to hold on to reality while her mind soared to unbelievable heights.

Breakfast. Should she fix English muffins or... *You have an exceptional talent.... You should think big.*

She rinsed Alicia's dinner dishes and put them in the dishwasher. She took out a grapefruit, sliced it in half and paused to stare at the little wooden swan on the windowsill. *Doing is living.*

Saturday. She had to hurry, she thought, as she began to section the grapefruit. She'd promised Lynn she'd be at the store early. The jumpsuit was finished, so maybe she'd bring...

You don't hide something like that in a place called The Boutique.

Launch a line of clothes. Well, why not? She could send her portfolio. No. Talk to Mr. Spencer first. No. Call George. *Really, Cicely, just who do you think you are?*

She started the bacon, took out eggs, wondered if she should call Alicia or take up a tray.

She couldn't approach that man again. She absolutely couldn't. The way he'd brushed aside the dress shop. But Mark said her mistake had been to approach a big man with a little idea.

As the bacon sizzled, she closed her eyes, trying to see clothes with a CICELY label in shops all over the world. She couldn't imagine it.

She opened her eyes to rescue the bacon just in time and placed the strips on a paper towel.

But above, beyond, overriding all was something else. Something warm and sweet and sensual, so unbelievable that her mind refused to grasp it. Touched it lightly and darted away. This incredible man had sat across from her and said incredible things that—

"Oh, I just love the smell of coffee and bacon in the morning." Alicia came in and immediately poured herself a cup of coffee, careful to push up the lace cuff of her frilly rose housecoat. "And Cicely, you have breakfast all ready. How nice."

"Yes." Cicely kissed her mother's cheek. "Sit down and eat your grapefruit while I get the eggs ready. Did you sleep well?"

"Oh, you know how it is when I'm alone at night. But I must have slept rather fitfully, for I didn't hear you come in. You were so late, Cicely."

"I—yes. Well, I called." Cicely popped the muffins into the toaster and managed to eat her grapefruit while she did the eggs. Over easy as her mother liked them. "Mr. Dolan took me out to dinner."

"That nice man who's taking Leonard's place at bridge?" Alicia paused with her spoon halfway to her mouth. "He was in Sacramento? That's strange. He lives..." She swallowed her grapefruit and shrugged. "Oh, well, he must have been there on business."

"Yes. I suppose. But he waited for me at the escalator and he said—"

"Still, I wonder what business it could be. He doesn't seem to do anything."

"Oh?" Cicely set their breakfast plates on the table and sat down to join her mother.

"I thought he was George's boss that first night, you know. Well, that is, I thought he was Mr. Simmons and . . . Cicely, these eggs are delicious. You always do them just the way I like them."

"Oh, I see," Cicely said, almost to herself, as she began to eat hurriedly. *George's boss called.* Cicely had called George's place and found that both he and Spencer were in Japan. "So you thought he was Mr. Spencer?"

"No. Mr. Simmons. And then . . ." Alicia frowned. "Well, he said he wasn't Mr. Simmons and I'm sure he said he was George's boss. No matter. He is charming. Where did he take you for dinner?"

"The hotel across from Grove's. The same place George took me to meet Spencer." And where I met *him.*

"Well, that was certainly nice of him. Cicely, dear, could you stop by the library before you go to The Boutique? I don't have a thing to read, and television is getting so boring."

"Sure. I really enjoyed talking with him. Mr. Dolan, I mean. He . . . he . . ." She hesitated, wanting to test the idea. "Well, he thinks I should approach Mr. Spencer about launching a line of my clothes."

"How nice. You'd better pick up some more of this strawberry jam, dear."

"Yes, I will. He thinks my designs are good. He seemed very interested."

"Now, isn't that just like the dear boy! He's so interested in everything and everybody. Even Ashley Trent." Alicia stopped spreading jam on her muffin to give a disparaging wave. "Tomatoes. Ash is a tomato farmer, you know, and Mark kept asking him questions. Imagine! Holding up a bridge hand to talk about tomatoes!"

"Oh." Interested in everything and everybody. "What does Mr. Dolan do?" Cicely asked, pretending great interest in her bacon and eggs.

"Nothing. I told you, he doesn't seem to have a thing to do. He's from London, you know, visiting his sister. On vacation, he says, but just between you and me, this so-called vacation is lasting a long time. And I haven't heard him say a word about leaving. He said he was writing. Or was it painting?" Alicia frowned. "Anyway, he said it was something he'd been wanting to do for a long time."

Do what makes you happy.

"Frankly, I believe he's just dabbling. Lots of time on his hands. Calls me at the oddest times and just wants to talk about the bridge column. But he does play a superb game, you know, and he's so charming. Everybody likes him. And very British. I just adore that British accent, and that darling way he has of calling all the ladies 'love.'"

All the ladies. Something twisted inside Cicely, and she felt suddenly dispirited.

"Even Josie Starks who's as sour as a crabapple. But when Mark flashes that smile of his and says, 'Now, what was your bid, love?' she just gushes with sweetness."

I'll just bet she does, Cicely thought savagely, leaving the table to rinse and stack the breakfast dishes. The same way I gushed last night. And I drank too much wine and let him fill my head with stupid fancies!

Well, come down to earth, Cicely, and get to work.

"Don't forget to stop by the library," Alicia called as Cicely started out. "Here, wait. You can take these two back. And do see if you can get any more by that Lela Jamison. I do love the way she writes."

"All right, but I'll have to do it at lunchtime. I promised Lynn I'd come early today." Cicely hurried out the door, clutching the books and draping the jumpsuit over one arm.

How else could she sell it except through The Boutique? She must get these stupid fancies out of her head.

However, Mark Dolan was no fancy. And he did seem, as Alicia implied, to have lots of free time. Twice that week, he turned up at the store just before one o'clock.

"Hello, Cicely. Can I take you to lunch?"

"Well, I brought a sandwich. I like to spend the time outside."

"Good. We'll walk down and get a shake."

It was a beautiful sunny day, and there were several people strolling through the outside mall or sitting on benches. Mark, Cicely decided, was just as comfortable sitting on a bench outside Macy's eating a hamburger as he was in a plush restaurant. Somehow, in spite of that excited expectancy he always aroused in her, she was beginning to feel more and more comfortable with him.

And, yes, she found he really was interested in everybody. Like the woman who shared their bench, and was having an argument with her young teenage son about a pair of outlandishly colored shoes he wanted to buy.

"Don't you think I'm right?" the woman appealed to Mark.

He didn't just smile and nod as almost anyone else would have done. He engaged in a long conversation with the woman about peer pressure versus parental authority. Clever, too, Cicely thought, the way he led the woman to decide for herself which things were important enough to argue about.

When Cicely left to go back to work, Mark was talking with a man who had just retired and complained that he "was bored out of his skull."

"Well, what do you like to do? What do you enjoy?" she heard Mark ask as she hurried away.

She supposed Mark was doing what he liked. Writing, not painting; the second time he met her for lunch, she'd asked him. "My mother said you were a painter. I thought you said—"

"Your mother has a remarkable capacity for getting things mixed up. Haven't you noticed?" His grin was good-natured, as he shook his head. "No. I'm not painting, I'm writing. At least I'm trying to."

"So you're a writer?"

"Not really. It's just something I've wanted to do for a while now. This is my first venture."

"What are you writing?"

"Oh, just about life and living. Kind of a guide to being happy. And you, Cicely—are you happy?"

"What? Why...yes, of course." Was she happy? She was surprised she'd never thought about it.

"And did you send your portfolio? Contact that chap who launches ships and things?"

"Well, no. Not yet." She frowned, ashamed to tell him she'd lost heart. Thinking maybe she *would* call George. Hardly realizing that Mark had diverted the conversation away from himself.

That night Lynn phoned. Someone had bought the lace dress. "Some blond woman who's never been in here before. She went absolutely bonkers over it. Didn't quibble about the price at all."

Six hundred dollars! Bonkers! No quibbling about...six hundred dollars! Maybe... Then and there, Cicely phoned George. Joanne said he was out of town, but she'd have him call as soon as he returned. Cicely began to think about what she'd say when he did call; meanwhile, she sorted through her portfolio, discarding this sketch, replacing it with that one. Maybe, just maybe...

Early Sunday morning, Mark phoned.

"Oh, I must tell you," she cried. "Do you remember that lace dress? It sold! For six hundred dollars."

"Did it really, now? Well, well. And just think—from a place called The Boutique. What do you think it would bring displayed in a Paris salon?"

"Oh, you're impossible!" she sputtered through her laughter. But she was beginning to imagine it now—clothes all over the world with CICELY labels on them. Maybe, just maybe...

"What do you do for fun, Cicely Roberts?"

"Fun? Oh, I..." What *did* she do for fun? "Oh, I read." When she had time.

"That's fine, but you need exercise, too, love."

"Well, I do get that," she said, chuckling. "As a matter of fact, I was just going out to pull weeds. The flower beds are—"

"Not bad. But I was thinking of something more stimulating. Do you play tennis?"

"Oh. Yes. I used to." She couldn't keep the enthusiasm from her voice. "When my father was alive." When there had been time and someone to play with.

"Good. I'll collect you in half an hour."

"Oh, I'm not sure I can."

"No time for arguments or persuasions, Cicely. We're scheduled for a court at ten. Doubles. And I promised to bring the fourth. See you directly. Cheers."

He certainly takes a lot for granted. I could be very busy. *Pulling weeds?*

That little flutter of excitement was already stirring, as she searched for her long-discarded tennis shorts and racket.

THE OAKS COUNTRY CLUB was larger and more plush than the small racquet club where Cicely had played with her father. It contained a golf course, an Olympic-size swimming pool and twelve tennis courts. Although her shirt and shorts were snowy white and spanking clean—she'd even pressed them—she felt positively grubby as she observed the mob of

people fashionably dressed in colorful sports clothes and
swimwear. Designer sports shoes. She was the only one
wearing plain old sneakers.

It seemed that everyone who wasn't playing or swimming had converged on the wide terrace that surrounded the
big clubhouse. Mark, smiling and exchanging greetings with
one person after another, led Cicely to a table that afforded
a very good view of the tennis courts. As they approached,
a tall dark-haired man stood up, and a young blond woman
flashed a dimpled smile.

"My sister, Lisa. And her husband, Richard Hartfield.
This is Cicely Roberts," Mark said, pulling out a chair for
her.

"Hello, Cicely," greeted Richard. "I'm glad you could
join us."

"And I hope you're not one of those expert tennis players," Lisa added with a grin. Her English accent wasn't
nearly as distinct as Mark's, obviously the effect of years
spent living in the United States. "For once," she was saying, "Richard and I would like to beat the pants off this arrogant brother of mine."

"Well, you've got a good chance, because I'm pretty
rusty," Cicely said, returning Lisa's smile. Dimples instead
of creases like Mark, she thought. And Lisa was petite while
he was tall. Her hair was lighter, too, but those hazel
eyes . . . *definitely brother and sister.*

"It matters not who wins or loses," Mark began but was
interrupted by Richard.

"As long as it's you who wins, you no-good bum. Like in
last week's tournament..." He shook his finger at Mark. "I
almost whomped you. If it hadn't been for that last set. I
was just plain worn out. Now, if I'd been lying around like
you all week, pretending to write—"

"Oh, do stop it!" Lisa gave her husband a playful slap. Or was it playful? "He's working for his room and board. He even took Donald to the dentist last week."

Mark grimaced. "And a very unpleasant chore that was. Guard your tongue, Richard. If I'm to continue to enjoy your hospitality—" He broke off, noticing that a waiter was standing by, and turned to Cicely. "Would you like a mimosa, love?"

"No. No, thank you. Just orange juice, please." Certainly not mixed with champagne. It would loosen her tongue exactly as the wine had. Keeping her head was already hard enough, with the laughter and chatter of people all around them and the continuous whack-thump of tennis balls, to say nothing of the banter that was going on between Mark and his brother-in-law.

Other people joined them, pulling up chairs or standing by the table, and Cicely's innate shyness surfaced. She felt absolutely tongue-tied, unable to murmur much more than a soft "how do you do." Lisa was kind, addressing most of her remarks to Cicely, but she seemed to be eyeing her in a speculative way, which made Cicely even more self-conscious. Mark also tried to include Cicely in the conversation, occasionally reaching out to touch her hand.

However, Cicely began to feel shut out, strangely intimidated by some of the women who stopped by in their provocative tennis shorts or bikinis. These women, it seemed, were determined to engage Mark's interest, impertinently tweaking his ear or rumpling his hair, making flirtatious remarks—"Say, you copped out on us the other night!" or "You promised you'd help me with my backhand. Now, when?"

Cicely withdrew, watching more in envy than anger, much as she'd watched girls like Debby in high school. She wished she could be that relaxed, that audacious and playful. She wished she could say something clever. She wished she'd worn something else. Well, that is, if she'd had anything else to wear.

She looked at the girl who had tweaked Mark's ear. Her baby-blue tennis dress with its halter top was smart and different. Interesting that white was no longer required on the tennis court. In fact, almost anything seemed acceptable, as long as it was short enough. Sports clothes. Now that was an idea. She began to sketch a tennis outfit in her mind. In traditional white. Short, with an A-line flare. Classic, understated and ... well ... sexy.

"Okay, our court's available. Come on, tiger. Let's get 'em!" Mark grasped her hand to pull her to her feet, and she saw that Lisa and Richard had picked up their rackets and were already going down the steps. Cicely followed, holding tight to Mark's hand, trying to remember everything her father had taught her. She'd played a good game once. She hoped she still did.

During the warm-up, she began to feel less apprehensive. After a few minutes of volleying, she found that her net game was as good as ever, though her ground strokes left much to be desired. She found she was hitting as well as her opponents, but none of them could match Mark, who was hitting casually and easily, like a pro. They lost the first set, and Lisa crowed with glee.

"Pride goeth before a fall," Mark declaimed, grinning broadly. "We're just setting you up. We'll take the rest."

They did take the next two sets. Cicely thought she was playing well. Her confidence grew, and she glowed every time she heard Mark's "Good shot, love."

She felt hot and flushed and vitally alive. It was good to be playing again, calling upon energy and expertise she'd forgotten she had. One more point and the fourth set would be theirs.

Lisa sent a ball spinning over the net, which Mark retrieved at the baseline with an excellent backhand stroke.

However, it was intercepted at the net by Richard, who returned a soft, lazy drop shot that Cicely lunged for, knocking off her glasses. She heard them crunch as she landed on her right foot.

A wave of desolation shot through her like pain. She stood there, dismayed and helpless. She couldn't see a thing.

CHAPTER SEVEN

"OH, DEAR! I'm afraid they're quite ruined. I'm so sorry."
That was Lisa, evidently picking up her glasses. "Do you
have a spare pair?"

"Not with me. And I'm sorry. I've ruined your game,"
Cicely said, her voice trembling with embarrassment.

"Nonsense. Our time's about up anyway." That was
Mark, his arm around her waist, gently taking the racket
from her clenched hand. "Let's go eat. I'm starving."

"Oh, wait!" Cicely cried. "There's glass all over." On the
court. Her fault.

"I'll take care of it," said Richard. She heard him call
someone to get a broom and then say, "Go on in and get a
table, Mark. I'll be right there."

Others gathered around, indistinguishable people who
murmured, "What's the matter?" "Did she get hurt?" "Do
you need . . . ?"

"Thanks. No. Everything's fine. Just a pair of broken
glasses. No, thanks. We're just going in to brunch," Mark
said, as he led her through the crowd.

"Mark, I think I should go home. I—"

"I know. You can't see. Don't worry, love, you're with
me. We've been through this before, remember?"

On the side of the terrace where brunch was being served,
there seemed to be less of a crowd, or at least, a quieter
crowd. She was surrounded by the murmur of low voices,
the clatter of silver against china, the smell of hot food and
coffee.

"Sit here, Cicely. It's a buffet. I'll serve you." Mark hesitated. "Lots of choices. Would you like—"

"The Spanish omelet is delicious," Lisa interjected.

"That sounds fine," Cicely said quickly. Anything. She couldn't get over a sense of acute embarrassment. She felt so helpless, sitting there, having to be waited on. She wished she could just go home. But she'd already spoiled their game; she wouldn't spoil their brunch, too.

"Thank you," she said to Mark, when he placed her plate before her.

"Wait," he told her. "I'm taking half of your omelet. And I'll give you ... maybe a fourth of my seafood crepe. There now," he said, as he completed these arrangements. "Eat up, champ. You didn't tell me you played such a spectacular game, Cicely. I think I'll make you my permanent partner."

"No, mine," said Lisa. "Listen, Cicely, there's a women's tournament next month. Will you be my partner for doubles?"

"And mess up just like I did today?"

"Nonsense, that was just an accident. A once-in-a-lifetime thing."

They were being kind, trying to put her at ease. Ignoring the fact that she'd broken her glasses and—

"Nearsighted, Cicely?" That was Richard, surprising her.

"Yes. I can hardly see without my glasses."

"You could get rid of them, you know."

Oh, no. She'd been through that before.

"I'm allergic to contacts."

"Yes. I imagined. Hard to fit contacts, anyway, in a case as difficult as yours."

"Oh." What did he know about it?

"There is another alternative. Have you ever considered radial keratotomy?"

"What's that?"

"A surgical procedure that corrects nearsightedness. It's commonly referred to as RK, and I'm surprised so few people seem to know about it."

Cicely's first reaction was a kind of wide-eyed wonder. Not to have to wear those heavy glasses she'd worn almost her whole life. Not to ever experience this kind of helplessness again. Not to be different. Her second reaction was disbelief. Did Richard really know what he was talking about, and if so, why hadn't she ever heard of this operation?

"Dr. Smith, my ophthalmologist, has never even mentioned it." She spoke tentatively, trying to remember when she'd last gone in to change her glasses. Surely he would have told her about the surgery.

Richard smiled. "Not all ophthalmologists use this technique."

"Why?"

"Well, for one thing, it's so new, and it requires specialized training. For another, we don't yet know whether there are any long-term side effects. And as with any surgery, there are risks."

"What risks?" she asked.

He launched into an explanation of the procedure, its possible risks and benefits, adding that the likelihood of success depended on the vision problem experienced by the individual patient. "In the majority of cases," he went on, "results so far have been good. If you like, you can make an appointment with me and we'll see whether you're a candidate for RK."

"Listen to my husband, Cicely," Lisa interposed then. "He's an eye surgeon. A very good one. And RK just happens to be his specialty."

"Oh. I didn't know." Cicely looked closely at Mark and caught the blurred image of a confirming nod.

"Yes," Mark said. "He certainly knows what he's talking about."

An eye surgeon. Mark had known it, and he hadn't told her. She didn't know why this irritated her. Why should he have told her? And why did she feel now as though she were some kind of specimen, as though she were on display, being examined? Cicely felt naked and exposed and more conscious than ever of being different. Still, she couldn't help but listen to what Richard was saying.

"This surgery—it must be costly," she ventured.

"Only about fifteen hundred dollars—"

It might as well be fifteen thousand, Cicely thought.

"—and it's covered by many health insurance plans," Richard explained.

But not hers, which didn't even pay for glasses. It was as if a door, suddenly opened to a beautiful vista, had been slammed shut in her face. And this, somehow, made her more keenly aware of her exposure, her embarrassment and frustration. The frustration expressed itself in anger, leveled at Mark. Anger that she concealed during the rest of brunch and the smiling goodbyes. Anger buried in controlled silence as Mark drove homeward.

"You're so quiet, Cicely."

"Yes."

"Are you angry about something?"

"No."

"I'm sorry about your glasses. You have a spare at home?"

"Yes."

"Good. And the lenses on these can be replaced." He reached over to touch the glasses, which Lisa had wrapped in a paper towel and placed on Cicely's lap. "The frames are just a little bent."

"Yes."

"Let me take them in for repair. Who did you say your ophthalmologist was?"

"Oh, stop talking in circles! Say what you want to say."

"Which is?"

"You knew about that surgery! That radia... whatever it is your brother-in-law does," she accused, her temper flaring.

"Yes, I did know about it."

"And you wanted him to tell *me* about it. That's why you arranged for us to play with them!"

"I certainly didn't arrange for you to break your glasses."

"I wouldn't put it past you!" She stopped, feeling a little silly. Then, almost sure he was grinning even if she couldn't see him, she plunged on. "You're so clever at arranging things. And it was very convenient, wasn't it? An excellent opportunity for Richard to tell me how I could get rid of these glasses."

"And you're ready to fight anyone who suggests that you take off your shield!" Mark shouted over the roar of the traffic, as he pulled out to pass a truck.

"And just what do you mean by that?"

"I mean you're hiding behind those glasses, Cicely. Because you think you can never be as beautiful as your mother. So you refuse to compete."

"Why would I want to compete with my mother?" she asked in honest astonishment. "I—I love my mother."

"Love her! You idolize... glorify her. You wait on her hand and foot. And denigrate yourself in the process. You hide from life!"

"That's not true!" Her glasses a shield? "I need my glasses to—"

"Forget those bloody glasses! They're just part of the facade. An excuse not to look your best. And an excuse not to be treated as an adult—as a woman. Think about it, Cicely. You design beautiful, stunning, exquisite clothes.

And yet every time I've seen you in public—except once—you dressed like you've been bargain hunting in a thrift shop. Making sure no one thinks you're trying to be beautiful!''

"You, of course, know exactly how I feel!"

"Very likely. Tell me, when you were a little girl, did you ever dress up in your mother's clothes?"

"Why—I . . . What's that got to do with anything?"

"Did you?"

"Well, no. But—"

"Aha! That says a great deal, Cicely, whether you know it or not. Most little girls—"

"I'm not most little girls. I'm me! And I don't know why we're back in my childhood, anyway."

"I'm sorry. You're right." He'd come off the freeway now, and was paused at a stoplight. "Listen, let's discuss this RK."

"Let's not discuss it. There's no point. In the first place, I don't have fifteen hundred dollars. And if I did have it, I certainly wouldn't spend it on some silly cosmetic surgery."

"Cosmetic. Ah, yes," he said as the light changed, and he drove on. "That's just how you'd view it."

"And how would you view it?"

"Correctional. You seem to forget that you're practically blind, Cicely."

Blind! No one had ever said anything so cruel!

"I am not blind! I can see perfectly well with my glasses."

"Without them, you're helpless. You stood on that tennis court today, and you didn't know which way to turn. And that night at the restaurant, when you sat down at my table, you couldn't even see me. You didn't know who the hell I was! I could have been anybody. I could have led you right out of that hotel!"

"Oh, no. That's ridiculous. I would have screamed, yelled for—"

"Oh, no. Not you," he declared, when he stopped in front of her house. "You're too ashamed to admit you need help. You don't want to depend on anyone. You're an insecure girl who's afraid to give *or* take!"

"And you're a self-righteous prig who talks like a shrink! Where did you get your degree in sidewalk psychology, anyway?" she shouted, as she jumped out of the car and stumbled up the steps. Thank goodness, the door was unlocked.

"Cicely. Wait!" She heard him run up the steps after her, heard his knock on the door.

She leaned against the door, breathing hard. He'd said... But she didn't want to remember what he'd said. Something—something that had begun to be wonderful—had been spoiled.

She waited. Finally she heard him go down the steps, get into his car and drive away. It was then that she moved.

"Cicely, dear! You're back? Good," Alicia called from the kitchen. "Here's George on the phone for you."

George? What did he want? Slowly, she made her way to the kitchen.

"Hello."

"Hi, Cissy. Joanne told me you called."

"Oh, yes. Well, it wasn't...isn't important." Nothing. Just something Mr. Do-what-you-like-and-be-happy brought up. What does he know?

"Not important? Joanne said you talked about showing your designs to Spencer. You know we never did do that, Cissy. She said something about starting a line of clothes."

"Oh, George. I was just...well, maybe thinking too big. Don't bother about it."

"Too big! Hey, kid, I think it's a great idea. Just the kind of thing Spencer would like to get his teeth into. And this town is running over with garment factories. Listen, Mom says you always have a lot of sketches. Can you send me some?"

"Well, I have a portfolio."

"Good. Put it in the mail right away. Spence will be back in the morning, and I want to catch him in between trips. Try to get them here before next week."

She said she would, but it didn't seem important anymore. She had lost her enthusiasm.

CHAPTER EIGHT

ALICIA, SAYING she'd spent a restless night, elected to stay in bed the next morning. Cicely took a tray up to her mother and ate her own breakfast of a boiled egg, sweet roll and coffee standing at the kitchen sink, fuming about Mark Dolan.

She didn't care if she never saw him again! He was a pompous self-righteous dictatorial jerk with an inflated opinion of himself. What did he think gave him the right to tell other people how they felt and how to run their lives? Especially considering the way he apparently lived his own life—sponging off his sister and brother-in-law.

Cicely hadn't wanted to believe it at first and had only half listened to Alicia's comments about him. *He doesn't seem to have a thing to do... vacation is lasting a long time.* But the banter at the tennis club with his brother-in-law... Had it really been joking? *If I'd been lying around like you all week....* No, it was no joke the way Lisa had rebuked her husband and slapped his hand. *Do stop it. He's working for his room and board.*

A grown man running errands for his sister?

She paused, deep in thought, before pouring herself another cup of coffee. He didn't act dependent at all. No, his very air was one of strength and assurance. A carefree, confident man with time and money to burn.

Just like her father! Oh, yes, she had seen it before. No one could have been happier or more carefree than Cecil Roberts. He laughed his way through life, enjoying his tennis, his bridge and his wood carving. He'd always done just what he wanted to do—and neglected the rest.

Do what makes you happy.

Let someone else pick up the tab—a sister or a father. Often, as a child, she'd heard her father make remarks that had been insignificant to her then. "Is that what you want to do, Alicia? Sure, we can afford it.... I'll just touch the old man for a loan."

Even after her grandfather's death, their lazy extravagant life had gone on. As she often found herself doing, Cicely picked up the little wooden swan from the windowsill. She rubbed the smooth wood against her cheek and remembered how much she had loved her father. How she and Alicia had leaned upon him, absorbing his strength, his generosity, his zest for life. Taking everything for granted, they'd had no inkling that he was on the verge of bankruptcy. The shock of that discovery had changed Alicia to a shell of her former vivacious self.

Mark had said she idolized Alicia, waited on her hand and foot.

And what do you know, Mark Dolan? You've never stood there, frightened and helpless, and watched Alicia coughing and choking, caught in the throes of an asthma attack that could easily snuff out her life.

Cicely looked down at her half-eaten roll, the coffee that had grown cold. She poured it out, then put her dishes in the dishwasher and hurried upstairs to collect Alicia's tray. She ran back up to take Alicia the novel she'd left in the living room and another mug of hot coffee, kissed her and went out to the car.

She drove down the freeway a bit too fast, thinking of a man with a gentle smile. A man who said cutting things . . . *You're hiding behind those glasses.*

Hiding! She thought of that day when she was...six? Hiding behind Stella's curtain, pulling it aside a little to watch the girls across the street, playing hopscotch.

"Why don't you go over?" George had asked.

"Don't want to," she told him. Because *he* was there. Emily's visiting cousin, a boy who had asked, "What's wrong with you? How come you wear those big glasses? Lemme try 'em."

"Sometimes," Stella had said, "kids aren't making fun. They're just curious."

"Uh-huh," Cicely had answered. But she didn't play with them again until Emily's cousin went back to Colorado.

She wasn't six years old now. She was a grown woman. And she wasn't hiding, either behind or because of her glasses! She was living her life, taking care of business, having fun.

She suddenly remembered the tennis game. She'd been having fun then; she'd felt clever and competent, part of the group, until... Again she experienced that sick feeling when she heard her glasses crunch under her foot. *You stood on that tennis court today, and you didn't know which way to turn.... You're practically blind!*

It was a cruel thing to say. All right, she had to concede it would be more convenient not to have to wear glasses. Still, that operation would be a long, tedious process, and she couldn't take the time off from work, even if she could afford the fifteen hundred dollars.

And she absolutely hated people who tried to ferret out the hidden secrets of a person's life. Especially irresponsible, impractical people like Mr. Know-it-all Mark Dolan. She pulled sharply into the parking lot, got out of the car and went up to work.

At noon, she took her sandwich out of her purse and started out, planning to take her usual walk.

He was there, waiting by the escalator.

Her heart fluttered crazily, as a tumultuous rush of feeling, warm and sweet and sensual, swept through her, catching at her breath, prickling her skin.

"Hello, Cicely."

"Hello." She felt awkward, ill at ease. And strangely happy.

But as they moved in silence down the escalator, through the crowd, past handbags and jewelry, her bitterness returned. Why had he come—to continue his tirade of cruel accusations? As they walked through the outer door into the sunny mall, she braced herself. She would not be intimidated by his pompous dictatorial utterances. She would tell him exactly what she thought. She—

He took her hand, pressing it gently. She looked up to see him smiling down at her, and the barrier she had built between them began to crumble. Together they wandered through the crowded mall, finally stopping at a bench outside a hamburger stand.

"Milk shake or soft drink?" he asked.

"Shake, vanilla." She glanced at the sandwich in her hand. She hadn't even brought her purse. Had she expected him to be there? To buy her a drink. How could he afford it—did he ask his sister for loans? She took a close look at him as he stood in line outside the vendor's window. He wore casual clothes, tan slacks and a short-sleeved cotton shirt. But her trained eye discerned that they were the very best cut, which meant expensive. And the soft kid loafers had to be Gucci. Maybe he had a private income.

"Are you planning to be here long?" she asked when he returned and handed her a shake. "I mean, here in the States?"

"Depends," he said, setting his drink on the bench and unwrapping a hamburger.

"Depends on what?"

"On how things develop. I'm just playing it by ear."

How things develop. The book or a job...or something else? She wouldn't ask. She certainly didn't intend to probe into *his* life.

"Cicely?"

"Yes."

"Yesterday, I really did take you to the club just to play tennis."

"I know."

"I thought...well, you're always so busy. I wanted you to have some fun."

"I know."

"Afterward...well, I'm sorry. I hope you'll forgive me."

"All right." She didn't know if he was asking to be forgiven for being a pompous jerk or for saying she was blind. Both of which were true, she thought, smiling a little. And suddenly it didn't seem to matter.

"Why are you smiling?"

"Oh, no reason. Nothing important. Something I thought of."

"I want to tell you something, Cicely. Something Richard told me," he said, looking down at his hamburger. "It's a true story. This chap was a correspondent for one of the networks, stationed in Lebanon, about two years ago. He was very nearsighted. He got kidnapped by one of the more fanatical groups. His glasses were knocked off and broken, and he became completely disoriented. Couldn't see his captors, didn't know where he was for a whole year."

"Oh." He had said it very simply. But she knew. She could feel the man's dilemma, his frustration. Lost and blind.

"After a year, he did manage to escape. I don't know the details. But after he got away, he came upon a group of people. He heard them talking, and he couldn't tell whether they were friends or enemies. He had to take a chance, and as it turned out, it was a lucky chance. But you do get the picture, don't you?"

"Yes." She stirred her drink thoughtfully, then looked directly up at him. "Are you trying to frighten me?"

"Oh, no, Cicely, don't think that!" he said quickly. He frowned. "It's—well, it's just that you referred to RK as cosmetic surgery. You seem to think that having it done would be succumbing to vanity."

"Wouldn't it? I'm certainly in no danger of being kidnapped."

"True. But you will admit that if the correspondent hadn't had to depend on his glasses, it would have . . . well, lessened his danger. Made it easier for him to cope."

"Of course. But, as I said, I am—"

"All right. All right. You will probably never be kidnapped. But put it this way. Years ago, thousands of people were crippled by polio. Now that it can be prevented, it doesn't make sense not to get the vaccination, does it?"

"No, it doesn't," she agreed. Suddenly feeling very lighthearted, she laughed. This surgery was corrective, not cosmetic. Vanity had nothing to do with it. It just made good sense. And to be free of those heavy glasses, she thought, lifting them to rub the bridge of her nose, would be . . . wonderful. "Maybe someday," she said.

Someday. Why did she say *someday*? He could tell she was convinced. Her eyes had lit up for an instant and then—

"Well," she said, standing up. "Back to work. Another day, another dollar."

Money. Of course. That was it. *Mark, you're a bloody fool. She doesn't have the money. Or, if she does have it, the very last person she'd spend it on would be herself. She's too independent, too responsible. And without an ounce of self-indulgence.*

"Wait!" he said. "I'll walk back with you. I want to tell you what I really came to say. It's Richard. He's looking for a volunteer."

"A volunteer?" she asked, as they hurried back.

"Someone who has a very severe case of myopia, such as yours, who will allow the surgery to be observed by some ophthalmology students. In which case, Richard will do the surgery free of charge."

"Oh." He saw her eyes light again, then darken. "I'm sorry, but I just don't have the time. I—I can't afford to miss work. I've just started, you know."

"Twenty minutes. That's all it takes. In his office. And for working people, he usually does it on Friday. So they can rest over the weekend and be back at work on Monday."

She stopped, turning to face him, hands on her hips.

"Twenty minutes? In his office? Then why does it cost fifteen hundred dollars, for heaven's sake?"

"Expensive equipment. Expertise. Insurance. I don't know...lots of reasons. But, listen, shall I tell him you're interested?"

"I'll think about it. Have to run now." She started to pull open the heavy street door, then turned back. "Thanks for the shake. And thanks for telling me."

"Sure," he said. He'd call her tonight, convince her. But first, he'd get to Richard and make the arrangements.

CHAPTER NINE

THAT EVENING Cicely Roberts did two things that were to markedly affect the rest of her life. She volunteered for the demonstration surgery, as Mark had suggested, and she packed up her portfolio of design sketches to be mailed to George the next morning.

After he'd examined her eyes, Richard confirmed that she was indeed an ideal candidate for the surgery. He told her it would be done one eye at a time, three weeks apart. She asked why she would have to rest in the hospital for three days after each operation. Mark hadn't mentioned that.

"So the students can observe the recuperative process," Richard said. "You wouldn't want them converging on you in your house, when you're supposed to be sedated and resting, would you?"

"No, of course not," she answered. And she certainly had no reason to complain, when she was getting this wonderful surgery, hospital and all, for free. She arranged for time away from work and hired Daphne, a teenage neighbor, to stay with Alicia while she was in the hospital.

"TELL ME, MARK," Richard said, as he stood in the guest house bedroom, watching his brother-in-law pack. "Why are you insisting on the hospital routine for this Roberts woman? It's really unnecessary. Patients can easily rest at home."

"Not this one," said Mark, pushing a sweater aside to cram a shoe into his suitcase. "If her mother wanted a cup of coffee, she'd jump out of bed, take off that eye patch and run to pour it.''

"Oh. Her mother's ill?"

"That's debatable." Mark lifted a batch of shirts from the bed and stood for a moment, wondering where to put them.

"Oh, I see. That kind. Here, let me." Richard pushed Mark aside. "You take care of the suits. You just might be able to get them on the hangers straight." He took out the shoes, sweater and socks, and began to pack, carefully and methodically. "Well, the hospital it is. You're footing the bill, pal." He shot a quick glance at Mark. "You do seem to be taking an inordinate interest in this young lady."

"Oh, it just bothers me when I see someone who's so obviously not putting her talents to use. Someone who's willing to settle for much less than she deserves." As he spoke, he straightened a coat with exaggerated care, not looking at his brother-in-law.

"Oh! Professional interest, huh? One of your how-not-to-live cases, perhaps to be cited in your book?"

"No, no, no, no, no. Cicely is...I could never think of her as a case." He paused, trying to define her in his own mind. So talented and industrious. So much care for her mother but never a thought for herself. And an elusive quality only briefly glimpsed, a joyful zest for life that had never been fully released but bubbled below the surface, lurking behind that tentative smile of hers. "No," he said reflectively, "Cicely is different from anyone I've ever known."

"So, I take it your interest is personal, then."

"No. No indeed. Not personal," Mark said emphatically, turning to look at Richard, who carefully concentrated on the sweater he was folding. "Certainly nothing more than friendship," he added. Cicely was too naïve, too trustful. And needy. No casual involvement for her. He knew she was inexperienced, knew she could easily be hurt.

Not at all the kind of woman he ought to be pursuing. Yet she'd somehow touched him as no other woman ever had.

He sighed. Yes, it was just as well that the book was finished and he was going back to work. Back to England. Far away from temptation.

ALICIA WAS even more excited than Cicely about the operation. "You'll finally be able to get rid of those horrible glasses! Of course, I'll be all right while you're in the hospital. It's just for a few days and then everything's back to normal." She had Leonard, one of her bridge cronies, drive her to the hospital each evening so she could make sure that "all was going well" and to remind Cicely to "keep still and do exactly what the doctor says."

Lynn also visited, and Cicely even received flowers from the other women in Alterations.

So why did she feel abandoned? Why did she feel expectant every time the phone rang, every time someone came to the door—and then disappointed?

After all, she'd only known the man for what? Two months? How, in that short time, had he come to be...a kind of support, a strength?

No. That wasn't true. He wasn't supportive. He was manipulative. No, bossy. That was it. Always telling a person what to do.

Do what makes you happy. Be a big designer. Don't worry about money.

Ha! Well, I don't have anybody to pick up the tab, Mr. Know-it-all!

Maybe that was it. Maybe his brother-in-law had kicked him out.

Cicely, that's mean! Why do you think such thoughts? He could be famous—writing under a pseudonym. No. He said this was his first writing venture. Well, no use conjecturing. The truth was that he'd been very private about himself and his affairs.

And very interested in mine! So why isn't he here with me during this surgery? He's the one who suggested....

No. He told you about an opportunity. And you should be grateful, Cicely Roberts. You've always wanted to be free of those glasses. Now she was—or would be, once the recuperative period was over.

The surgery itself hadn't been bad, despite her fears. The three days' rest in the hospital was like a vacation. Nothing to do but listen to music, sleep and be waited on.

And there were flowers from Mark. Both times. He had thought of her. He did care. But the flowers with their two short notes were not enough to make her hope. She could read nothing but friendship in the hastily scrawled words: "Thinking of you. Hope all goes well. I'll see you when I return."

She hadn't even known he was gone. Or where. The note said he was coming back. But when? A month...a year from now?

She pushed him from her mind, and went on with her life. She certainly didn't need Mr. Mark Dolan. Not for support or strength or...anything else.

The operations were successful. For a short while, her eyes were sensitive to glare, and Dr. Hartfield insisted she wear eye patches at night so that she wouldn't rub them. But after a month, all traces of the surgery were gone, and her eyes no longer filled or burned.

It was wonderful! For the first time in her life, Cicely could see herself without glasses, the lines of her face clear and straight. She touched her cheek, staring at herself in the mirror, reveling in the wonder.

She could see everything! When she woke in the morning, every detail of her bedroom came into focus—dresser, pictures on the wall, shoes askew on the floor. Her bedroom was no longer a blur—like something seen through a frosted window—while she groped for her glasses. Nothing was a blur now. She could move about, work, *see*, without that heavy appliance resting on her nose. She could hardly explain the feeling.

"It's like going barefoot," she told Lynn that first Saturday when she went back to The Boutique. "Without the glasses, I mean. It gives me a kind of freedom."

"A freedom that might be enhanced," Lynn said, looking her over critically. "Do you know, you could be beautiful, Cicely."

Cicely only laughed. Vanity was an unfamiliar habit and in any case, she'd always associated beauty with the peaches-and-cream, blond perfection of her mother. Certainly not with her own olive complexion and thick, unruly black hair.

It was Lynn who dragged Cicely to a beauty salon to have the black hair fashioned in a new layered cut that fell smartly to her shoulders. But it was Alicia who got out her cosmetic case and suggested this lipstick and that shade of blush, and perhaps just a touch of eye shadow.

Here Cicely balked. No shadow, no eyeliner; nothing was to come near those precious unencumbered eyes.

"Oh, honey," Alicia coaxed. "Now that we can finally see how pretty your eyes are, why not make the most of them? Just watch what a little mascara can do to those lashes of yours. Don't worry. I'm being careful. Hold still. Now. Isn't that better?"

Cicely gazed at herself wonderingly. Her lashes seemed longer and thicker, her eyes dreamier. And she saw something else with surprise and pleasure. Those indentations, the little red marks on each side of her nose, were gone. Her face was smooth and clear. "You're quite an expert at this," she told her mother. "You've made me look...well, almost pretty."

"Very pretty," Alicia said with a proud smile.

But it was more than a new face. It was a new feeling of companionship, a connection—as if wearing her mother's cosmetics made up for something she'd missed as a child.

For the first time in her life, Cicely began to experiment with makeup. And something prompted her to find the time to whip up a couple of dresses for herself, to buy a pair of frivolous high-heeled sandals. On impulse, she even made the tennis dress she'd sketched in her mind that day at the club.

Despite the new freedom, life for Cicely went on much as it had before. Soon after Cicely's last surgery, Alicia caught a chill and spent the next two weeks confined to her bed, even canceling the bridge sessions.

"We have to be so careful with any kind of bronchial infection," Cicely told Lynn, "because of the asthma." Again she hired Daphne to come straight from school and stay with Alicia. Cicely spent almost every moment when she wasn't working caring for her mother, coaxing her to eat, reading to her, making her comfortable.

Luckily, Alicia was out of bed and back to her normal self when Cicely received the phone call, early one Sunday morning.

"Tennis anyone?" asked a husky British voice.

Cicely felt as if her heart was caught in her throat. She couldn't utter a word.

"Cicely? Are you there?"

"Yes. I thought... Oh, Mark, you're back. I didn't know."

Mark hadn't either. Hadn't known how one person could haunt him. His usual tendency was to become involved with a person—with people—in a detached sort of way. Yes, he often tried to drop a hint or two if he thought it would help someone to get more out of life. But it had always ended there. He'd watch and listen and maybe make a suggestion. Then he'd move away, go on with his own affairs.

But Cicely... Not even with a continent and an ocean between them could he move away. He couldn't shut out the memory of her haunting blue eyes, the little gurgle of laughter that delighted but always surprised him. Her busy little hands with the short unpolished nails. Her bare feet. He would feel an erotic quickening of his pulse, whether he was having lunch at his club or tramping through the woods. Even in the midst of a session with one of his patients. A sudden ache, a disconcerting sense of how much he missed her, would suddenly sweep through him.

"I have to go back to the States for another couple of months," he told his partner, when the request for revisions came from his editor. "Where I'll be free of distractions." Back to the peace and quiet of his sister's guest home. Back to Cicely. He wanted to be face-to-face with her, where he could sort out his feelings. And hers.

SHE WAS SITTING on the porch steps waiting for him, racket on her lap. As he drove up to the house, she immediately sprang to her feet and hurried toward him, an expression of open excitement animating her face.

"Hello, Cicely." With an effort, he kept his voice normal, noncommittal. She looked so fresh and vibrant, like a schoolgirl, in an outfit that was... well, uniquely different, combining a sophisticated stylishness with youthful simplicity.

"One of your creations?" he asked.

"Yes." Her grin was shy. "I had planned to take it to Lynn next Saturday. But when you called..."

"Keep it for yourself. It suits you."

Surprisingly, he missed the glasses. The thick lenses had magnified every fleeting expression, clearly revealing every unspoken thought. Now her expressions were quickly veiled by her long thick lashes. He'd called her glasses a "shield," but without them it was as if the inner Cicely remained somehow hidden from him.

Cicely's hand tightened on her racket as they drove toward the club.

Just friends. A friendly game of tennis. Nothing more.

She couldn't make bantering or witty conversation. But she could be friendly in a calm, impersonal way. If she tried very hard. The weather—that was always a safe subject.

"It's been unusually hot so far this summer." Good, her voice sounded light and casual.

"Very pleasant in London," he said. "Lots of rain, though."

London. So that's where he'd been. For what? How long would he be staying here this time? She refused to ask.

But he asked her questions, about work and about Alicia, and of course, about the operations. When she said she now felt free, he smiled and said, "Like going barefoot?"

He knew. He understood. Some of the easy camaraderie returned, a camaraderie that was broken the minute they entered the clubhouse and a crowd converged upon them. No. Upon him.

Cicely moved aside. The new sense of freedom, the new appearance, had done nothing to allay her innate shyness. She instinctively withdrew, deferring to women she considered more attractive, more interesting.

However, this time Cicely attracted some attention herself. There was a young man named Ross, who insisted on buying her a coffee and engaged her in conversation until he was reminded by one of his golf buddies that it was "tee" time. Several women gathered around Cicely, too, more intent on finding out about her outfit than about her. "Really different...so quaintly original...wherever did you find it?"

When she revealed that she'd made it herself, it caused even more of a sensation. "Could you possibly make one for me? Maybe just a little different...maybe in blue?"

"Sorry," she said. "I have so little time." She had vowed a long time ago that she would never be what Stella had been, a personal seamstress for several clients. Women who knew exactly what they wanted until they tried on the finished product, which never seemed to suit. Poor Stella.

No indeed, Cicely had no intention of trying to please these fashionable, exacting women. "I'm sorry. I couldn't," she kept saying, feeling more and more intimidated, and glancing around for Mark.

She finally saw him, and her heart gave a little lurch. He was away from the crowd at another table. Alone with a woman. She was blond and beautiful and she wore one of those provocative French swimsuits that revealed more than it concealed. Mark was leaning intently toward her. She was smiling up at him. Being, Cicely knew, charming and clever.

This time, something more than envy stirred in Cicely's breast, something primitive and fierce. Her cheeks burned, her heart pounded, and she felt an almost uncontrollable urge to run over and grab that blond hair and yank it hard.

She was appalled at herself! We're friends, she repeated over and over, just friends.

MARK HAD BEEN SURPRISED when the woman approached him, addressing him as "Dr. Dolan." Crystal—what was her last name? How did she know who he was?

"It's my business to know," she assured him. "I'm a PR consultant. But don't worry. I won't expose you. Not until I'm ready to launch you, that is."

"Launch *me*?"

"Yes. You—and your wonderful book. Don't you want to be rich and famous?" she asked coyly.

"Not really."

"But you do want people to buy your book?"

"I want them to read it."

"Well, if you want your book to be widely read, you'll need exposure," she said.

"Oh, but the publishers—"

"I've worked with them before. If you're agreeable, they'll give me a contract to promote your book. Didn't your editor call you?" Mark shook his head, slightly bewildered.

"Well, you'll probably hear from him tomorrow."

"How did you know I was going to be here at the club?" Mark asked suspiciously.

"I called the home number I was given and spoke to your sister," she answered. "Don't worry, everything's legitimate. In fact, this contract would be ideal for me since I live in the Sacramento area—and I even belong to this club. So we'll be able to work closely together. Very closely." She touched his hand and her smile was full of admiration. "Your book is pretty special, you know. And considering today's rage for self-improvement—well, it could become quite a success. With my help."

She began talking rapidly of television and radio interviews, autographing sessions, personal appearances. He was a little stunned. He'd expected to write a book and go straight back to work. He started to explain that he didn't have the time, but she interrupted.

"Just give me a month," she said, leaning toward him and stroking his arm seductively. "You'd be surprised at what I can accomplish in a very short time. Especially if we plan well in advance. But I'll need your consent, of course, and your cooperation. Now, let's see. Your publication date is..."

He made no promises. In fact, he listened with only half an ear. His mind was on something else.

He was imagining Cicely in England, wandering barefoot through his familiar rooms, kneeling on the floor to sketch her designs. In that completely absorbed manner of hers. She was still so young. Younger, he sensed, in experience than in years, no matter how industrious and creative she might be. Consumed by a sudden and tender feeling of protectiveness, he looked across the terrace at Cicely.

She was talking with a group of people, willing herself, or so it seemed, not to glance his way.

"I'll think about it," he told Ms. Crystal Morris, taking the card she had produced from somewhere. He wondered about that; no room for a pocket in that swimsuit of hers. Yes, he told her, she could call him at home to arrange for another meeting, and leaving her, he went to Cicely.

His game wasn't up to its usual standard. He was too busy watching Cicely. Seeing the light in her eyes, the way she put her heart into the game, exerting every muscle, bringing forth another glimpse of that zest for life.

They drove home in companionable silence and he held her hand all the way. He walked with her up the steps and into the house, cool and dim after the outdoor heat and blazing sun.

Carefully he set her racket down on a small table, then pulled her gently into his arms, and touched his lips to hers. The sudden yielding as she melted against him sent his senses reeling, triggering a yearning deeper than he'd ever felt before. He pressed her closer, devouring her with his kisses, intoxicated by the warmth, the sweetness of her.

"Cicely, dear? Is that you?" came a plaintive call from upstairs.

He could not stop the hungry exploration of his mouth, his hands. It was Cicely who finally pulled away.

"Yes, Alicia."

"Oh, good! I thought I heard you. It's George. On the phone."

Damn that George!

"For you, Cicely. He seems rather anxious."

"All right," Cicely murmured, backing away from Mark. "I'll take it in the kitchen."

Blast that woman! Mark paced the hall. And blast all this modern communication—intercoms and telephones. Again, he fleetingly pictured being in England with Cicely, at the manor house...in their private quarters. He had wandered into the living room when she returned, her face aglow with excitement. An excitement that had nothing to do with him.

"He likes them. He likes them!" she cried.

"Who?" What was she talking about?

"The sketches. Remember? You told me to send them to Mr. Spencer, and George says he loves them!"

"Oh."

"And he likes the idea—your idea, Mark—of launching a line of clothes. He's sending me a ticket to come to New York to talk about it and...I can't believe it...a contract. That was George on the phone. He's making all the arrangements. Can you imagine it? Fashions designed by Cicely Roberts! Oh, I have some more ideas. Some sketches upstairs. I'd better get them ready to take with me. Oh!" She gave a little twirl, then turned to him, her face alive with exultation. "You made it possible, you know. You told me to ask him. To send the sketches. Oh, thank you, thank you!" She gave him an impulsive hug. A hug that had nothing to do with love or passion.

CHAPTER TEN

GEORGE HAD SAID she should come as soon as possible because Spencer was leaving for Europe the following week. Thursday was her day off. If she took Friday off from Groves and Saturday from The Boutique, she should be able to do it. She arranged with George that she'd leave on Wednesday evening and return Sunday night.

On Tuesday during her lunch hour, she found a perfect gray gabardine suit on sale in the store's designer shop. The gray kid pumps weren't on sale, but the cost wasn't too bad with her employee's discount. If she was going to talk to Brick Spencer about launching a line of her fashions, she ought to at least look like a fashion designer. She was glad Lynn had made her get the haircut.

When George called to say that the only Wednesday night flight he could get was out of San Francisco, Mark offered to drive her there.

"We'll go down early and have dinner," he added. "This calls for a celebration."

Alicia clearly had mixed feelings about the whole enterprise, wishing Cicely luck in one sentence and bemoaning her absence in the next. "What will I do if this cough starts up?" she wailed more than once.

"Now, don't worry," Cicely would reassure her. "Dr. Davison says you're doing fine. And Daphne will be with you the whole time—thank goodness for summer vacation! And she's promised to help you get everything ready for your bridge on Thursday. Anyway, before you know it,

Sunday will be here and I'll be back." Cicely carefully instructed Daphne about Alicia's medications and her breathing machine—just in case—and left the girl a list of emergency telephone numbers.

Mark was to pick Cicely up directly from work on Wednesday. So she carried her bag to work and got a ride with a fellow employee. She thought she was all prepared for the trip until she saw the black velour jumpsuit displayed on the mannequin.

"I must be going crazy," Cicely muttered to herself as she tried it on. But the jumpsuit was a perfect fit, and she couldn't resist it. It would be so comfortable for the plane ride, she told herself, yet smart enough for her arrival in New York. Crazy, perhaps, but she was glad she bought it when she saw the appreciation in Mark's eyes.

Cicely would never have called the two-hour drive to San Francisco Airport romantic, for that was a word, a thought, to which she was unaccustomed. Nevertheless, that was exactly the way she felt, even though she didn't know exactly how to express it. She was totally oblivious to the traffic, aware only that she was seated close to a handsome, dynamic man who had become very special to her. And his eyes, his voice and the occasional touch of his hand told her that she was just as special to him. The day itself seemed special, too, she thought, relaxing in the late-afternoon warmth as they sped by the hills of California, parched and golden in their summer garb. Cicely watched the boats bobbing in San Francisco Bay, and marveled at the most beautiful sunset she had ever seen, all yellow and red and gold, glinting against the silver bars of the Bay Bridge.

When he stopped in the airport parking lot, Mark took something from his pocket and turned to face Cicely. "For this special occasion," he said, handing her a small jewelry box.

"Oh, Mark!" She was hardly able to breathe when she saw the heavy gold pendant, rounded in the shape of a heart and suspended from a slender gold chain. "It's beautiful," she said, blinking away surprising and unexpected tears. She touched the carefully engraved *Cicely* in the center, like a signature that had been hastily scrawled by her hand.

"Do you like the logo?" he asked.

"Logo?"

"Your own personal signature on all those beautiful clothes you're going to design."

"Yes. Oh, yes." Now she could almost envision it—garments in shops all over the world, labeled with her own personal signature.

"You," she said, looking up at his smile, and because she couldn't help herself, tracing a finger along the endearing crease in his cheek. "You make everything seem possible." Then she was in his arms, his mouth against hers in a kiss that sent a wave of ecstasy spinning through her. An ecstasy mingled with gratitude, tenderness and the vision of wonderful possibilities looming ahead.

Cicely's exultation didn't wane during the candlelight dinner in the plush airport dining room. She could only toy with her food, so enthralled was she by the man who sat across from her. Totally unaware of the hours that passed, she was shocked to hear him say, "Almost departure time. We'd better get out of here." She saw him motion for the waitress to take the check.

Cicely sipped a little more wine while they waited—she could sleep on the plane—and smiled at him.

The waitress finally returned, whispering something to Mark, who looked surprised. "I don't understand," he said, not bothering to lower his voice. "There must be some mistake. Try it again."

"I tried it three times, sir, and it was rejected each time...authorization denied. I'm sorry. Perhaps..." The waitress hesitated. "Perhaps your limit has been exceeded?"

"Limit?" Mark looked as if he didn't understand the word. "Look, I'm sure there's some mistake. Could you call—"

"That's impossible, sir. I'm sorry." The waitress looked embarrassed.

"Oh, all right. I'll call myself tomorrow and give them hell!" Mark himself looked more exasperated than embarrassed. Cicely played nervously with her fork, as she saw him shake his head and exclaim, "This is ridiculous. All right. I'll give you a check."

Cicely suffered with Mark, watching his frustration increase when the waitress explained that they couldn't accept an out-of-town check without the clearance of a major credit card.

"And there's no talking to a bloody mixed-up computer," Mark muttered, as he dug in his pocket and pulled out all the money he had. Thirty dollars.

"Oh, Mark, let me," Cicely cried, reaching into her new leather shoulder bag. George had said she wouldn't need money, but she'd brought along a hundred and fifty dollars, just in case. "It's time I treated you anyway," she declared, handing him…what did he need? Fifty-five dollars?

"Thank you, love," he said, quite casually. "I'd hate to wash dishes. But I only need twenty-five. I have thirty."

"As if I'd let you drive all the way back to Sacramento without a penny in your pocket," Cicely said and insisted on paying the whole bill.

Cicely kept her smile bright, as they walked from the restaurant and on to gate 31. She wanted to save him from embarrassment—not that he seemed embarrassed. Even when the waitress told him of the rejection on his credit card, he'd seemed more puzzled, more irritated than humiliated. Could this be something he was accustomed to? People who lived hand to mouth...

"This chap who's meeting you in New York? He's a...close friend?"

"George?" she asked, startled out of her reverie. "Oh, yes. Very close."

"Oh." She saw his lips tighten, noticed the strain about his eyes. She'd been wrong; he *was* feeling humiliated, she decided and he was trying to hide it. She began to talk rapidly, lightly, wanting to put him at ease.

"It'll be good to see them again. Of course, George has been back and forth, but I haven't seen Stella in ages. Stella's his mother. She's the one who taught me how to sew. And I have yet to see the baby."

"Baby?"

"He and Joanne have a baby boy, about six months old now."

"Oh. I see. This George is married. Very close friend...good. He'll look after your interests." Mark was smiling now, his mood apparently improved. He cheerfully secured her boarding pass and gave her a light kiss when they parted. "Have fun. And hurry back to me."

Hurry back to me. The words still echoed, as she sat by the plane window, staring out into the night at the flickering lights of the airport. She felt very dispirited.

Because of a credit card rejection?

No. Because it tipped the balance. Because it made her realize that the suspicions she'd harbored and refused to believe were probably true.

It was all a facade. Mark Dolan, who gave every appearance of being strong, dependable, *responsible*, was underneath...irresponsible. Undependable. Like her father...
For a moment she was swept back into the miserable months after her father's death, the shattering revelations, the struggle just to survive. She had felt so lost, so destitute.

She felt that way now, as if something beautiful had been snatched away from her. She'd been on the verge of...falling in love? She thought of his clear, discerning eyes, the laughter in his voice, the feel of his hand on hers.

He'd even made the eye operation possible, had somehow known what it would mean to her. He'd prompted her to send the sketches that were opening up these wonderful opportunities for her. Now she could...

Do what makes you happy.

A rush of tender compassion swept through her, and she felt utterly miserable for him. Was *he* doing what he liked? Was *he* happy? *Oh, Mark,* she thought. If only he could combine some of that philosophy with practicality, think more of himself, and not so much of other people!

So generous. She touched the locket at her throat. *Probably not even paid for yet.*

Like her father, who'd given them everything. It was only after his death that they learned how insecure the foundations of their happiness had been.

Mark Dolan, I could love you. And I was beginning to think you loved me.

That, too, could be a facade. Just because he's the only man who's taken an interest in you doesn't mean you're the only woman who's ever interested him! You saw those women at the tennis club, converging around him, acting so familiar. And let's face it, he left you for at least half an hour and sat with that blonde...and it seemed to be a pretty intimate conversation. Perhaps she...

She wouldn't think about that. It meant nothing to her. She could never give her heart to a man like Mark. Even if he should ask.

"CISSY! WHAT HAPPENED?" George burst out when he met her. "Where are your glasses?"

Cicely told him about the surgery.

"Well, well, here's to modern medicine. You look great. Not just the glasses, but the new hairdo and the makeup! I always knew you were beautiful. Now maybe you'll believe it, too. Spence was impressed when he saw you in Sacramento, but baby, just wait till he sees you now!"

Cicely smiled, pleased with George's praise. But she said she was there to promote her designs, not herself.

"And that's going to be some promotion," George said, as he led her to his car. "Just wait till you hear what's happening!"

New York was a different world, she decided, as they sped along the freeway.

Dirtier. Uglier. Busier.

Older, Cicely thought, as George maneuvered his Porsche across a weather-beaten iron bridge, one of the network of bridges spanning the various muddy waterways. She remembered reading somewhere that New York City was made up of five islands and—

"I just can't tell you how impressed Spence is with your sketches," George shouted over the roaring traffic. "He's really got big plans. We've set up several meetings, to cover as much as we can while you're here."

"That's good." Cicely tried to recapture some of the excitement and enthusiasm she'd felt when George had first phoned her. Now she just felt scared and inadequate. Overwhelmed by the movement and noise, the screeching of brakes and blaring of horns, as trucks and cars and taxicabs swerved in and out of lanes. Was the old bridge sturdy enough to hold all this traffic?

"I'll take you to your suite first," George was saying. "You can freshen up, and then we're going to meet Spence at the office."

"Good. I'm really anxious to see him and talk over what he wants." Cicely spoke brightly, determined not to act like the country bumpkin she felt. Now they'd crossed the bridge. The river was still on their right, but on the left, she saw tall brick apartment houses. Taller than the ones in California, and built much closer together. No shrubbery, but she did see little strips of lawn. They drove through a long tunnel, and finally they were on the streets of Manhattan.

But the noise and rush of traffic didn't abate as they negotiated the narrow streets, hemmed in by tall buildings. Everywhere hordes of pedestrians hurried past or wove their way across a busy street. The people all seemed to blend together in an almost indistinguishable mass. And they all seemed to be carrying umbrellas. There was an umbrella stand on nearly every corner, as well as food stands with charcoal burners, the food and the burning charcoal producing a strange distinctive smell that permeated the whole area.

"After the meeting with Spence, we'll move on to the Waldorf for lunch with Sue Ellerby."

"All right." Among the crowd Cicely noticed several tall, slender, exquisitely dressed women, who strode purposefully past. Models, she guessed, by the identifying bandboxes swinging from their hands. They were stunningly chic, from the smart hats perched on their heads down to the *tennis shoes* on their feet. Cicely began to giggle. Somehow the sight of those practical tennis shoes on women who might someday model her fashions made her feel more relaxed.

Then they were on the Avenue of the Americas, wider than most Manhattan streets and enhanced, surprisingly, by several well-placed trees. George relinquished his car to the parking attendant, and whisked Cicely up to the hotel where she was to stay. He told her that she'd be in the executive suite he always reserved for visiting dignitaries.

"I'm a visiting dignitary?"

"I told you Spence is impressed! He's excited about this big new venture he's starting—different from anything he's done before. And you're the key to the whole plan. So take that awestruck *you-mean-me?* look off your face, and get ready to wheel and deal. This is the big time, kid!" He grinned, then gave her a sudden quick hug. "You don't know what you're in for, do you, Cissy? But don't worry, I'll be here with you."

No, she didn't know what she was in for. She'd expected to have a short interview with Spencer, and then go out to visit Stella and Joanne, and see the baby. But she never did get out to George's Long Island home. Every day she was whirled from one session to another, all strictly business.

If she'd been awed by Brick Spencer when she met him in Sacramento, it was nothing to what she felt when she saw him in his own setting. From the moment she entered the high-rise building of steel, glass and marble that housed Spencer Enterprises, she was engulfed in an atmosphere of wealth and power. In the hushed elegance of his penthouse executive offices, luxuriously appointed with plants, priceless works of art and expensive furniture, she was led across a plush, thick carpet into the president's office.

"Ah!" he said, rising from behind his massive desk to greet her. "Here is the lady who diverted me with talk of a little dress shop, while keeping her real treasures hidden. How nice to see you again, Cicely."

"I . . . yes. Hello," she managed.

"You're just in time," he said. "We'll go right in."

In the conference room, seated at a long table with George, Spencer, his secretary and two other assistants, Cicely learned how much groundwork had been done before her arrival. They consumed cup after cup of coffee, and between telephone interruptions—Hong Kong, Mr. Spencer. . . It's Anchorage, sir, about the Alaskan oil lease. . . Johnson on the line from London, sir—they talked about everything from production costs to advertising, citing details she'd never even thought of. Cicely felt lost amid all the expertise and knowledge they exhibited, and overwhelmed by the magnitude of the whole project.

Then there was the luncheon at the Waldorf. Beautiful crystal chandeliers, large urns with gigantic arrangements of colorful flowers and shrubs...and tall, stunning Sue Ellerby, who would coordinate the spring showing. Except for the seamstresses they'd have to hire, Sue was the only person besides Spencer and Cicely who would be allowed a glimpse of the fashions before the formal showing.

"Secrecy is imperative, my dear," Sue told her. "So much competition and too many fashion spies." It was she who suggested that it might be a good idea for Cicely to continue working at home. "I've already engaged a location for the showing, and I'm making up a list of the buyers we'll invite. Now, let's see, our marketing target is the upper-echelon working woman, so..."

Cicely felt a little dazed by the rapid pace at which things seemed to be moving. By Saturday, when she met with the graphic artist, her head was pounding and she felt she was being carried along, willy-nilly, by a tide of plans and events that had nothing to do with her.

"The name is the thing," she heard Spencer say. "It has to be catchy. Let's see, what would catch the eye of our woman executive?"

Suggestions rapidly followed. Cicely sat quietly while the talk hummed around her. By this time, she had become so intimidated that she was almost afraid to open her mouth, certain she would say the wrong thing. She listened as names were proposed...Career Fashions, Executive Classics, California Classics... Slightly giddy, she put her hand to her throat and touched the gold locket. The cool, solid feel of it steadied her, and she remembered Mark's words: *Your own special logo.*

"If these are going to be my fashions," she said suddenly and perhaps a little too loudly, for everyone else became silent. She knew they were all looking at her, but she took a firm grip on the locket and continued. "Then they should bear my signature."

The graphic artist was impressed. "Yes," he said. "Simple and elegant." And Spencer agreed. Cicely sat up a little straighter, surprised that they'd gone along with it so readily. But then she thought, why not? It *is* my project! She experienced a heady new sense of confidence and found herself chatting quite naturally as they wound up the meeting.

Saturday night, Spencer took her to see a recently opened musical that had been garnering rave reviews. Cicely was enthralled by the music, the dancing and the beautifully dressed people in the audience. When they left the theater, it seemed that everyone who had attended the performance was standing on the sidewalk vying for a cab. She expected the chauffeur-driven limousine that had dropped them off to arrive at any moment. Instead, Spencer took her arm, and they walked for a few blocks until they reached a line of horse-drawn carriages. He ushered her into the first one and spoke briefly to the driver.

Cicely was amazed at how calm these New York horses were, apparently unperturbed by the noisy, honking traffic that veered around them as they clopped through the streets of Manhattan. The carriage finally stopped in front of an all-night restaurant near the hotel, and after a quiet candlelight dinner, Spencer accompanied Cicely to her suite.

"Aren't you going to offer me a nightcap?" he asked.

"I'm sorry. I don't have anything," she answered, a bit flustered.

"Oh, yes, you do." He showed her a cabinet that turned out to be a tiny refrigerator, holding wine and liquor, sodas, mixes and an assortment of cheeses and cold meats.

Then he pointed out another cabinet that contained nuts, chips, crackers. "Now, what will you have?" he asked.

"Nothing for me, thank you," she stammered.

"Oh, I'll fix you something you'll like," he insisted, smiling. "Something pleasant and not too potent." He quickly prepared a drink and handed it to her. "Try this."

She took a sip. It was delicious, tasting of tropical fruit and a hint of rum, neither too tart nor too sweet.

She nodded. "I do like it," she murmured, as she watched him pour a Scotch for himself.

"Tell me, Cicely of California," he said, sitting on the sofa and reaching for her hand to pull her down beside him, "what do you think of your project?"

"My project!" she stammered. "It's your project more than mine. I never, never imagined all this." She waved her hand. "It's...it's stupendous!" Suddenly she felt overwhelmed and inadequate again. "I...I hope it's successful."

"Oh, it will be." He laughed. "Everything I do is successful."

She knew it was true. His power and prestige, his confidence and business acumen—that was no facade.

"Do you remember how I told you I always survey the whole picture, all the possibilities, before I undertake any project?"

"Yes, I remember." She turned her glass around and around. This project was centered on her, her sketches and designs. She felt her stomach tighten with nervousness. It was already August and the show had been scheduled for April. She had eight months to create...how many outfits? Could she do it? Doubt balanced precariously with elation, and she faltered. "I—I'm very grateful for this opportunity, Mr. Spencer."

"Brick."

"Oh, yes. Brick. I...well, I'll try not to disappoint you."

"Oh, you won't." He spoke with such certainty. "I've seen your sketches. And I know I'm going to enjoy working with you, Cicely."

"I hope so." She smiled a little uneasily. There was something about the way he was looking at her....

"And I hope you're going to enjoy working with me," he said smoothly, placing his drink on a side table.

"Oh...oh, yes, I will."

"Things are a bit rushed this time, because I'm leaving for Europe on Tuesday. But you'll be making frequent trips here, and I hope the next time you come, we'll have more time for pleasure." He took the glass from her hand and put it on the table. "There will be more evenings like this when we can enjoy ourselves." He leaned toward her and twisted a lock of her hair around one finger.

Abruptly she got to her feet, feeling there was something she should set straight. But she didn't want to seem ungrateful, or act like an unsophisticated greenhorn. Or give the impression that she thought he intended something...when maybe he didn't.

"It's been a delightful evening, Mr. Spencer, and I've enjoyed it so much. But it's rather late now, and—"

"And you don't mix business with pleasure," he said, standing and smiling down at her. "Very wise of you, Cicely Roberts."

"Oh, no," she said, shamefaced. "I wasn't... That is, I don't...didn't think—"

"That I was coming on to you? Don't be too sure." He rubbed her cheek with the side of his thumb. "I find you very appealing. But that is quite separate and apart from your talents as a designer. In other words, my dear, I never write my contracts in the bedroom."

"Oh" was all she could say. But she felt the hot blood rush to her cheeks.

"You're quite right. It is late," he said, as he walked to the door. He opened it, then turned to face her. "I should warn you, however, that I never allow business to stand in the way of my pleasure. I plan to see a great deal of you when I return."

"Oh. Yes."

"Good night, Cicely of California," he said with a chuckle. Then he went out, closing the door behind him.

CHAPTER ELEVEN

GEORGE HAD ARRANGED Cicely's return flight to Sacramento, where she arrived early Monday morning. She called home from the airport, and Daphne told her that Alicia was still asleep and that everything was going well.

"Good. Just tell Alicia that I'm back and I'll see her this evening," Cicely said. Then she took the shuttle into town and went directly to work.

"Surely you're not going back to doing alterations," George had said. "You won't have time. Besides, your contract includes a monthly salary that isn't exactly peanuts. To say nothing of your percentage once we start selling. You're in clover, Cissy."

"I know. And I know how much of my good luck is due to you," she'd told him, giving his arm an affectionate squeeze. "I appreciate the way you've protected my interests. And I won't let you down. I plan to do a good job. But," she added, "I have to give notice so they'll have time to replace me." George could not know what the Groves job had meant to her, coming at a time when both her finances and her confidence were at rock bottom. She would not leave them in the lurch.

So she reported for work at ten, saying nothing to anyone about her new project, adhering to Sue's "keep it quiet" warning. She did go up at noon to give two weeks' notice or less if they could find a replacement.

She began to make her own plans, too. She knew she would need the help of a competent seamstress, maybe two, if she were to meet Sue's April schedule. She would check with Ann Levinson, a middle-aged woman who did occasional work for the alterations department. Cicely was familiar with Ann's skill and remembered that she'd said she didn't want to make the daily trek to Sacramento from Roseville, where she lived not far the Roberts house. She wondered about Dan, her friend from design school. What was he doing? If she could get in touch with him, would he be interested in making pattern drafts? She worked steadily, her head full of plans that had no relation to the hems she was letting down or taking up.

Although it wasn't a particularly grueling day, it was difficult for Cicely, with her fingers flying one way and her mind another. Also she'd traveled all night and had to adjust to the east-to-west time change. By seven o'clock, when a fellow employee dropped her at home, she felt completely drained.

"Oh, Cicely." Alicia looked up from the sofa where she sat with Daphne, watching television. "Why haven't you called me? Daphne told me you were home this morning, and I thought surely you'd call me during the day."

"I'm sorry. I did mean to call, but things piled up. It's been a long day." Cicely put down her suitcase and bent to kiss her mother. She paid Daphne, who seemed anxious to depart, then turned to Alicia. She wanted desperately to go right upstairs and fall into bed, but she also wanted her mother to know what had happened, to share their good fortune.

"Oh, Alicia," she said, "I have so much to tell you. You just can't imagine." The words started tumbling out. "Mr. Spencer—Brick—was so impressed by my designs that he's launching a line of my clothes. Fashions by Cicely. We're introducing them at an April showing. In New York. You'll have to come! Everything's already been set in motion, and— I'm ecstatic! Just ecstatic." She paused for breath.

"Cicely, that's wonderful! I'm not surprised, either. Your father always said you were talented, and he knew about these things. But honey—" Alicia gazed at her plaintively "—I'm so glad you're back. I've hardly slept a wink since you left. And that girl's cooking doesn't compare to yours. I hardly ate any supper."

Cicely looked closely at her mother; Alicia's lovely face did seem paler, more haggard. "Why don't I fix us a snack?" she offered instantly. "Some cheese and toast, a cup of tea?" Despite her exhaustion, she bustled about preparing the light meal. They ate at the kitchen table and Cicely described New York—the constant activity of the streets, the excitement of the theater, the beautiful hotel room. But she could tell that Alicia was getting too sleepy to concentrate on the conversation.

In a matter of minutes she'd settled her mother in bed with a book and another cup of tea, then returned to the kitchen.

After clearing away the dishes, she started back toward the stairs, and noticed the mail on the hall table. Bills, still unopened. Well, with the new salary, she could easily pay everything. She picked them up, planning to slip them into her purse so she could take care of them tomorrow during lunch. She noticed an envelope from the office of Dr. Richard Hartfield and opened it curiously. It contained a bill marked Overdue, a bill that detailed the cost of the RK surgery. It amounted to $1498.45.

Overdue? She had been told that the operation was free. There must be some mistake; she would call the office in the morning. She didn't like being misinformed, but it occurred to her that if a mistake *had* been made, at least now she could pay for the surgery, perhaps through installments.

But she'd spent three days in the hospital each time and had received no bill from them. Oh, well, she was too tired to think about it now. She'd call Hartfield's office in the morning and see what was what.

Cicely tossed restlessly during the night, too high-strung to sleep. At breakfast, it seemed that Alicia was more fretful and demanding than usual. The coffee was too strong, the scrambled eggs too soft...and would Cicely run up and get that novel on her bedside table before she left for work?

Why, oh why, couldn't Alicia do just one thing for herself, Cicely thought irritably, as she went dutifully up to fetch the book. Then she was angry with herself. She shouldn't blame Alicia just because she felt pressured. Something wonderful had happened and she ought to feel happy, not overwrought. If she planned carefully and took one step at a time, things would work out.

But she still felt tired as she drove to work, almost feverish with excitement. So many ideas buzzed in her head, ideas she could hardly wait to execute. She hoped the store would find a replacement soon. And she had to talk to Lynn, possibly tonight. She would just tell her that she'd be too busy for the Saturday work and wouldn't be able to bring in any consignment clothes for a while. She felt guilty about not telling Lynn her plans; Lynn had always been supportive and would be glad of her good fortune. Well, after the launching in April, she'd be able to explain.

The launching! Cicely Roberts, you have arrived, she sang to herself, pleased with the designs stamping themselves on her mind. She was going to be successful—successful doing what she did best. What made her happy.

Mark. *Do what makes you happy.*

She touched the locket at her throat, and for a moment was consumed by thoughts of him. That lazy charming smile, the crease in his cheeks, the perceptive hazel eyes. She'd call him tonight and tell him what had happened and she'd thank him again. It was he who had planted the seed, urged her to take the chance; surely that made it all right to tell him. She'd just have to swear him to secrecy.

During her coffee break, she called Dr. Hartfield's office to straighten out the confusion about the bill. His receptionist was most apologetic.

"I'm so sorry, Miss Roberts. There's been a terrible mistake. You weren't supposed to receive a bill. Mr. Dolan gave us a check, then Dr. Hartfield told us to tear it up. But the girl had already put the information into the computer, you see, and somehow, it went out with the overdue accounts. I'm sorry. But don't you worry about it. Just ignore it."

"Thank you." Cicely hung up the phone, her mind focusing on one sentence. "Mr. Dolan gave us a check, then Dr. Hartfield told us to tear it up."

Mark had lied to her. He had paid for the operation. Or at least intended to pay, except that his brother-in-law refused his check. He must have paid the hospital, too. She touched her locket, remembering that night, less than a week ago, in San Francisco. The waitress returning his credit card, telling him authorization had been denied.

Credit. She knew all about credit. Her cheeks burned even now as she recalled the day... was it just two days after her father's funeral? They'd come and repossessed the car. How could she have known that he was three payments behind? And that wasn't the only overdue bill. She'd paid everyone out of the insurance money. It had seemed the only honest thing to do. But she had vowed she would never live beyond her means. She would never be obligated.

And now...?

Hers had not been a demonstration surgery, free of charge. It was all a lie, concocted by Mark, and carried out by Richard, who knew his brother-in-law didn't have $1498.45.

Maybe Mark only gave him a partial payment.

Oh, Lord! Whatever he gave him, Richard knew Mark didn't have it and was sponging on him as usual. And making her sponge! She felt humiliated, placed in an impossible position.

All right. The surgery had been wonderful. She was glad she didn't have to wear the glasses anymore. But...she could have waited.

Well, she could pay now. She would call Dr. Hartfield and tell him. No, she would tell Mark.

But, all at once, she didn't want to see him.

When she came out for lunch, he was standing by the escalator, his cheeks creased in that cheerful smile. He looked confident, responsible. But she knew it was all a facade, and she felt very depressed.

"Hello," he said. "I called yesterday, and the girl staying with Alicia told me you were back. I thought you might be tired, so I didn't call last night. But I can't wait any longer. How did things go in New York?"

"Very well." She spoke through tight lips. New York seemed long ago and far away. She was tired, angry, bursting with things she wanted to say to him. Undecided how to begin. All right, his intentions were good. But he had misled her.

"You don't look as if things went well," he said, easily keeping pace with her rapid stride through the store and out into the mall. "Let's find a quiet spot to have lunch, so you can tell me all about it."

"I'm not hungry."

"Wait a minute!" He seized her by both arms, and turned her to face him. "What's wrong with you?"

"You lied to me, didn't you?" She jerked away from him, oblivious to the people strolling past.

"What?"

"That RK surgery. It wasn't a demonstration surgery, was it?"

"How did you find—?" He checked himself. "I mean, what makes you think—"

"Never mind that." His readiness to deny what she already knew made her even angrier. "You paid for it, didn't you?"

"Well, not really. I—"

"Oh, that's right! You didn't pay for it. You conned your brother-in-law into doing it for free."

"Conned him? Oh, Cicely," he said, taking her arm, urging her to move on. "It wasn't like that. Richard didn't mind."

"I mind. And you shouldn't have lied to me!" She noticed a woman looking rather apprehensively at her and resumed walking.

"Oh, come on, Cicely." He spoke softly as he walked beside her. "Isn't this a bit of a carry-on? You needed the surgery and—"

"Not really. It wasn't as if I couldn't see at all. With my glasses—"

"Believe me, love, you needed desperately to come out from behind those glasses. In a case like yours—"

"A case like mine?" She halted again and turned to glare up at him. "Are you suggesting that I'm some batty lame-brained female about to have a nervous breakdown over a pair of glasses?"

"No, no, no, no, no! I didn't mean anything like that. You certainly are levelheaded, Cicely. If anything, too levelheaded. I thought—"

"*You* thought. You have a rather meddlesome habit, Mark Dolan, of telling people what to do about their own lives. What about what *I* thought?"

"You didn't seem averse to the surgery."

"I thought it was a demonstration—a kind of mutual favor. I didn't know you'd begged Richard to—"

"Ah, Richard was glad to do it! He's got tax problems."

"I'm not a tax writeoff. And I'm not a charity case, either," she said, walking away from him.

"Oh, come, Cicely." Mark followed her, adding placatingly, "Honestly, Richard was glad to do it. He couldn't care less about the money."

"Well, I do. Can't you understand that I don't like the idea of *taking* from anybody!"

"Exactly. You can take care of yourself, is that it?"

"Well, I can!"

"And heaven forbid that you should ever be dependent on anybody for anything, eh?"

"Let's just say I relish my independence. And that I'm quite capable of looking after myself." She sensed his growing irritation but was too angry to care. "Just because you thought my glasses were so unsightly that—"

"I didn't give a damn about those glasses!"

"Then why did you trick me into an operation that neither of us could afford?"

"You don't know a bloody thing about what I can afford!"

"I have a pretty good idea about what you *can't* afford. When a man's credit card . . ." She stopped, hand over her mouth, appalled at herself.

"What? Oh, you're talking about San Francisco. That's right. You bailed me out, didn't you?" He was actually grinning. As if it were a minor incident, something that happened all the time. "Here, let me reimburse you," he said, reaching for his wallet.

"No! I don't want your money!"

"Surely you don't think I'd let you pay for your own celebration. But thanks for the loan." Still smiling, he started to hand her some bills.

"No." She pushed his hand away. "I don't want your money. That's not what I'm talking about."

"Then what are you talking about?" Now he looked puzzled.

"I'm talking about overextending yourself. And...oh, Mark, I don't want you to do that on my account. I don't want you to—"

"Overextending myself? Listen, it was all a mistake. You don't understand."

"But I do. I understand more than you think. And...oh, I don't want to talk about it. I have to go." She turned, almost running, and hurried back the way they had come. She had said too much. She didn't want to hurt him. She didn't want to love him. But the anger had deserted her, and she blinked back tears, feeling the void, the emptiness.

"I THOUGHT I was doing you a favor," Richard said, when Mark confronted him in the kitchen. "Want a sandwich?"

"No, I don't." Food was the last thing on his mind. "What I want to know is who blabbed about that favor to the very person from whom I expressly wished it to be kept secret?"

"Nobody blabbed. It was all a mistake." Richard cut thin slices of ham with the expertise of a practiced surgeon. "It went out with the overdue accounts."

"Overdue? I left a check at your office, and you told me—"

"That I tore it up! Right. Professional courtesy and all that. Besides which," he added as he reached into the refrigerator for mustard and a tomato, "when one's dearly beloved seems concerned that her brother is destined for perennial bachelorhood, and when said brother exhibits an interest—however impersonal—in a young lady...well, one likes to give it a push, so to speak, and—"

"Will you cut the extraneous chitchat and tell me what the hell happened!" Mark shouted.

"Well, it seems that my very competent clerk had already fed the pertinent data into the computer, and—"

"Oh, lord, I don't believe it." Mark sank onto a stool and stared at Richard. "I know the things aren't supposed to have minds of their own, but I think they have a grudge against me."

"Oh?" Richard looked up from the sandwich he was assembling.

"I was the victim of a computer foul-up in San Francisco just the other night."

"Really?" Richard asked, as he seated himself beside Mark and bit into his sandwich. "Yes, I do see your point," he said, highly amused as Mark related the incident. "Fetch me a drink, old boy, while I mull this over. I take it the same young lady was somehow connected with both computer errors?"

"What are you driving at?" Mark asked, as he popped open a soda and set it in front of Richard.

"Just diagnosing the symptoms. Loss of appetite. Acute irritation over two minor infractions. Tell me, how do you feel? Is there a sense of outrage at this undue persecution by computers? Or is there a sense of being misunderstood? Unappreciated? Do you feel rejected by the young lady in question?"

"I feel that you ought to stick to your own field of incompetence!"

"Just trying to help you sort things out." Richard laughed. "I detect inordinate concern over minor—"

Mark slammed the door as he strode rapidly out.

But he knew he was more irked at himself than at Richard's teasing analysis. He tried to reason out why he was so annoyed by something so unimportant, something that could easily be explained away. He paced restlessly about the sitting room of the guest house, questioning himself.

He came to a sudden halt, as something buried deep in his subconscious clamored for attention.

Sybil. Gorgeous, vivacious, tempestuous Sybil. How he had loved her. How she could tear him apart. That last year had been riddled with her tantrums and wild accusations. She'd harbored suspicions about his female patients. He remembered the stormy confrontations whenever an emergency call interrupted a date, whenever he spent a harrowing night with a suicidal patient.

Now he could see Sybil for what she was—petulant, willful, selfish. But at the time, he had been young, very intense and deeply in love. He'd been desolate when she left him for a shipping magnate who "cares more about me than he does about other people."

He'd been completely over Sybil for years; in fact he rarely even thought of her anymore. But now he wondered if she'd made him wary, if the experience had left him unwilling to risk closeness with another woman. Had he indeed taken refuge in "other people," immersing himself in their problems, their needs? Neglecting his own?

He wandered into his study, dropped into the big leather chair and leaned back. There was something different about Cicely. Something so natural and endearing. So trusting.

He sat up. She didn't trust him! One little credit card foul-up and she was ready to doubt his integrity... well, at least his economic status. What did she even know about him?

What have you told her about you?

Mark stirred in his chair. He had spent almost every minute that she could spare with Cicely. They had shared so much.

She shared. Her problems. Her dreams. You pulled them out of her, didn't you?

Because I cared for her.

But you never allowed her to share yours.

He thought about that. Had he become what Lisa always called him—a people-watcher and people-listener? An observer of life? Never a real participant? Keeping himself insulated, uninvolved . . .

He had never told Cicely about himself. His work, his book, his life. Because once he had loved too deeply and been hurt. After all this time, he was still afraid to take the risk.

He looked down at the manuscript on his desk, the title page exposed. *Life Is for Living: A Guide to Happiness.* Wasn't this a case of "Physician, heal thyself"? His mouth twisted into an ironic smile.

TWO EVENINGS LATER, Lisa came into his study.

"I would have a word with you, brother dear."

"Oh?" Mark leaned back in his chair and put down the phone. Not home as usual. Well, he'd have to track her down at Groves again. He glanced up at Lisa, who had perched on his desk and was regarding him critically.

"Yes, you really are rather handsome," she decided, dimpling, her eyes dancing with mischief. "A bit of a slob, though," she added, brushing a lock of hair from his face. "Do you know you need a haircut?"

"Lisa! Will you get on with it?"

"All right. All right. Cicely called me yesterday and we had lunch today."

"You did!" He sat up. But then he remembered. "She wanted to figure out how she should pay for that surgery, huh?"

"Oh, yes, that." Lisa waved her hand airily. "But I convinced her Richard would be hurt if she offered more than a thank-you note or maybe a small gift."

"Good."

"But that, I gathered, was not her main concern."

"No?"

"What I was trying to tell you, dear brother, is that—charming and handsome though you are—your main attraction for most women seems to be your money."

"Lisa!"

"And I find it refreshing indeed to meet a woman who loves you, even though she seems to be convinced that you're a penniless bum and, I'm afraid, a bit of a leech."

"Cicely? She said that?"

"Oh, no. She was extremely careful *not* to say it. Let me think. What did she say?" Lisa pursed her lips as Mark watched in appalled silence. "I think she said you were generous, kind, so understanding...so thoughtful of others. And then she lapsed into generalities. How some people are so concerned for other people that they neglect their own affairs. And though she took great pains not to say it, I gather she thinks you're one of these people, giving to such an extent that you're on the verge of financial ruin."

Mark stared at Lisa.

"She deduced all that from one credit card foul-up?"

"Credit card?" Lisa looked puzzled. "She didn't say anything about a credit card. No, I gather it was just a general impression. Your long stay here. Your seeming lack of gainful occupation. And now that I think of it," she added, with a mischievous smile, "she may have misconstrued some of Richard's chance remarks."

"You know, Lisa, I just may throttle that husband of yours!"

"Don't blame Richard because you've formed the habit of keeping yourself to yourself."

"Me! It was *you*, dear sister, who insisted on secrecy until I finished the damn book."

"All right. Don't get upset. I came to give you this." She waved a check. "Five hundred dollars. She wasn't sure what you paid the hospital, but I gather she didn't want you strapped for funds on her account. She was almost certain you wouldn't take it from her. And, if you won't take it from me, I am to keep it until you really need it."

"No?" he said, looking at Lisa. Seeing Cicely. Industrious, independent, concerned for him. He was touched beyond words. And he wanted to shake some sense into her!

"Well, there you have it, brother dear. Will you enlighten her?"

"Maybe." He grinned. "Maybe not."

CHAPTER TWELVE

SHE MISSED HIM. She hadn't known it was possible to miss anyone so much. How could she have grown so close to him and become so dependent upon his companionship in just a few short months?

And now, it had been a week. No, almost two weeks since they had that angry confrontation. She felt lost. And ashamed. She looked down at the little tubes of paint she was putting into their case and wished she could unsay what she had said that day.

She'd felt so tired and so angry; it was only later, when she'd time to think rationally, that she realized how unfair she'd been. How unkind. Realized that everything he'd done, he had done for her.

She walked over to pick up her sketch pad, glancing around the workshop, trying to decide what else she should take. She hoped Lisa had said the right thing, and that she'd persuaded him to accept the money.

Money isn't enough! You should go to Mark yourself. Apologize for what you said. But she was too ashamed.

Too ashamed? Or too vulnerable? The way he gazed down at her, the way he smiled, the way she felt when he... She didn't want to think about his kiss. She didn't want to be in love with him.

But, lord, how she missed him!

She put everything into a canvas tote bag and took a last look around. She remembered how Mark had looked around that day, touching everything, praising her designs and her sketches. He'd been so interested. No, she wouldn't think about him!

She went down to her room for her keys and wallet. Then she hurried across the hall to check on her mother.

"Where are you off to now?" asked Alicia, who was sitting up in bed with a novel. "I hardly ever see you anymore."

"Just up into the hills to sketch some wildflowers. I'm trying to get some ideas for fabric designs."

Turning to look at her mother, she noticed that Alicia's face was rather drawn. Cicely hesitated, wondering if she should leave her, after all. Or maybe it would do Alicia good to get out for a while.

"Look, why don't you come with me?" she suggested. She'd wanted to get an early start and this would delay her, but . . . "I'll run your bath. And while you dress, I'll pack a lunch. It's lovely out. You'll feel better in the fresh air."

"Oh, honey, I'm really not up to it. I'm feeling a bit poorly. And I don't think I should tramp through the woods with my allergies. I wish you weren't going today."

"It won't be for long. I'll be back before dark. I left chicken salad in the fridge for your lunch, and Daphne said she'd come after school to check up on you."

Alicia gave a martyred sigh. "It's hardly the same thing. Are you *sure* you have to go? I'd been so hoping we could spend some time together."

"Yes, I have to go," Cicely answered, more curtly than she'd intended. She fought down her impatience. "We'll have a good long chat after supper. And I'll show you my wildflower pictures." She stroked her mother's forehead. "Now you have a nice restful day and don't fret. I'll be back before you know it." Quickly, before she could change her mind, Cicely picked up Alicia's breakfast tray and her own canvas bag and left the room.

Perhaps, she thought as she went downstairs, it was time she looked for a housekeeper. Someone who could take over some of the household chores and be an agreeable companion for Alicia. We can afford it now, she told herself, rinsing and stacking the dishes. She filled a plastic bottle with water, got an afghan off the sofa and went out the front door, locking it behind her. She'd just started down the porch steps when a car stopped out front. A familiar car. She saw Mark get out and come up the walk toward her. Halfway down the steps, the afghan over her shoulder, the bag in one hand, the bottle in the other, Cicely stood still, fighting to catch her breath.

What could she say to him? How to apologize?

Then he was at the bottom of the steps, looking up at her, his cheeks creased in that teasing smile, the steady hazel eyes appraising her.

"Just tell me one thing, love," he said, chuckling. "Why on earth are you wearing shoes?"

"Oh. Not shoes. Not really. Just my grubby old sneakers." Laughter bubbled in her throat, and she felt the tension drain from her. It didn't matter. It didn't matter about her old jeans and faded pullover. Everything seemed irrelevant. The angry words. Explanations and apologies. None of it mattered. He was here.

"Oh, Mark!" she cried happily. "I've missed you."

"And I've missed you," he said, taking the bag and bottle from her. "Where are we going?"

"We? Oh, well, I was planning to drive up in the hills to sketch wildflowers."

"Another five minutes and I would have missed you again, huh? All right, then. Come along."

She followed him to his car, and watched as he stored her things in the trunk. He told her that every time he'd phoned, she was out, and when he went down to Groves, he found that she no longer worked there.

"The only way to catch you is to barge in at an inopportune time." He glanced at his watch. "Like nine o'clock in the morning. You are a very elusive lady."

"Just busy. Oh, Mark, I've got so much to tell you."

"One thing you can tell me," he said, when they were seated in the car, "is why we're going up to sketch wildflowers."

"To get ideas for fabric designs."

"Oh?"

"Mark, I'm a designer! Oh, don't look at me like that. I mean really. I'm recognized now! So George could get me into the fabric mills, and . . . Oh, wait. You don't know. I'd better start at the beginning." The words tumbled out, all the things she'd been wanting to tell him. What had happened in New York and what she had done since returning. A whole day going through the fabric houses in San Francisco. "But I knew that was a waste of time. I'd heard years ago that the big designers snatch the best fabrics at the mills before they even get to the retail houses. So I called George and he arranged for me to get into several mills back east. I spent two whole days and I got several bolts. But the most fantastic thing I learned was that I could have fabrics made and woven exclusively for me, in whatever design I want."

"That's good," he said, smiling at her enthusiasm, but concentrating on the traffic.

"You say that so casually. Do you know what it means, how important it is? I used to search through thrift shops trying to find the right materials, and I'd have to use appliqués to get the color combinations I wanted. And now . . . My father was right. He said the best ideas come from nature. So that's why I'm going. Oh, I just hope I can match the colors."

"Color?" He glanced toward her and frowned. "Don't you think you'll find things rather drab up in the hills? It was dry all summer, and there've been a lot of fires."

"It was September the day my father and I came up here. I remember, because school had started and I was doing a project for Girl Scouts. You see, my father liked to do wood carving, especially birds. That day he photographed birds, and I collected wildflowers and painted. He'd given me a little paint box. We spent the whole day together." She was quiet, remembering the flowers and the little creek with its colorful stones.

"You miss your father, don't you?" He reached over and took her hand. "Did you spend many days like that, roaming the hills?"

"Oh, no. That was the only one. You see, Alicia wasn't interested in outdoor activities, and Dad was always so busy. But that day he pointed out so many things to me. He had a real feel for beauty. That's the only time I remember spending a whole day with my father. But it was fun and I got my badge for the project." Her voice faded. Only Stella had been there when she got the badge; her parents had been away on a trip. Even now she felt the loneliness, and she spoke quickly, as if to deny it. "Dad and I played a lot of tennis, though. We'd go out early in the morning, maybe even three times a week."

Early in the morning before Alicia got up, Mark thought. Even though she didn't say it, he heard it—the loneliness. He gave her hand a little squeeze. He hadn't known her father. But he knew Alicia. So self-absorbed that she wouldn't sense a daughter's needs. Beautiful Alicia. Yes, a man who had "a feel for beauty" could be completely bewitched by her. There would be little time left over for a child. And such a child could easily be intimidated by a tiny scar or an ugly pair of glasses, by some small flaw that assumed monumental proportions. Poor lonely little girl.

"Turn here," she said excitedly. "I think one of the fires was in this area."

Obediently, he turned off into a side road. They were in the foothills now, and yes, he could smell it, that acrid lingering smell of a long-burned-out fire. He drove for a while, and then he saw the actual site of the fire. It presented a strange and startling contrast. On the periphery were tall pine trees and underbrush, still green and healthy, surviving because of the wide firebreaks that had been cut. Then, on the other side, was the overwhelming expanse of the burned-out area. He felt a little sad as he looked at the tree stumps, charred and ruined, the land barren and destroyed.

"Oh, look! Stop. See, there it is. Fireweed! That's one of the things I'm looking for."

He stopped the car and followed her when she jumped out. Yes, he did see it now—the clumps of glowing orange among the ruins.

"Dad was right!" she exclaimed. "He said it got its name because it's one of the first plants to appear upon the blackened scars of a forest fire."

He smiled because that sounded so poetic, and because it gave him a thrill to look at the plants. Blazing with color, growing from the dead rubble. Surviving.

"Let's get my things. I hope I can copy it." Cicely took out her bag, and Mark spread the afghan in a cleared space. Then she set to work, talking all the while. "See! Dad said nature has the most beautiful combination of colors. Who would ever have thought of putting that lilac purple and fiery red together?"

Caught by her excitement, Mark took a closer look at the plant. Long stems, with spikes of lilac purple, brilliant rose or white, against the orange-red leaves. He sat beside her and watched, fascinated, as she mixed tubes of paint and water in little disks. "I want to get that exact shade of lilac," she said.

By mixing blue and red? he thought. And now she was adding white. And, by Jove, it was coming out purple. No, lilac, he thought, as she added more white.

"Is this it? Or this?" she kept asking, as she dabbed the mixture on the pad. "I'll just get the shade, and the shape of the plant. The design I'll sketch at home."

She was so vitally alive, so absorbed in what she was doing. Like that night in her workshop, draping that piece of muslin. Confident and vibrant. A woman who had blossomed, like fireweed, from the scars of a lonely childhood. A woman he loved.

Did she love him? Lisa said she did. And Lisa was pretty perceptive about such things. Oh, lord, that reminded him. The check. He'd come over this morning with the intention of returning it to her. And telling her the truth about himself. And it had all gone out of his mind. Everything had, except seeing Cicely. Just being with Cicely.

He stood, and walked quietly around, careful not to disturb her. They needed to talk. He would be going back to England in six weeks, and he wanted to make plans for their future. He wanted to ask her to go with him. He glanced down at Cicely, on her knees now, bending over her pad, that gleaming black hair falling about her face. She was so happy in her career that was just now coming to fruition. Could he ask her to leave?

Oh, hell, England had nature, too, he thought, grinning to himself. And London was no farther from New York than California was. He would get rid of the tourists and build her a studio in the east wing of the manor house. Plenty of early-morning sun there. But too far for him to commute every day. Well, they could get a town house in London, with space for a second studio. Anything. Anything she wanted, if she would only come with him. They would talk when they returned to her house. When he had her full concentration.

They drove about from place to place, and Mark was surprised to see so many colorful wildflowers and weeds, sprouting among the craggy rocks of the Sierra foothills. Around two o'clock, however, he announced that he was starving and they returned to the highway to find a hamburger stand.

"After we finish lunch, I just want to go to one more place," Cicely said, as she hungrily munched french fries. "Bear River. The water is probably very low now, and at the bottom, there are these pretty stones." So again they drove back through the hills until they found it.

"That's a river?" he asked, standing on the high bank and looking down at what seemed a shallow creek.

"Oh, yes!" she cried. "By next month, the water will be up to here."

But now they jumped down from the bank and spread the blanket on the sand, which in winter would be the bed of a swollen river. She was right about the stones. They were about the size of grapes, worn smooth and in various shades, so muted he wasn't always able to identify their true colors. Through the clear water, they gave the appearance of a soft, subdued mosaic.

"Aren't you going to paint them?" he asked, noticing that she had taken off her shoes and was wading through the water, her jeans rolled up.

She shook her head.

"Oh, well, if it's time to play..." He grinned, pulling off his own shoes and rolling up his jeans. He felt the water cool on his feet as he splashed toward her.

"But I'm not playing," she said, staring up at him and backing away as if startled by something in his expression. "I was going to collect— Oh!" The exclamation broke from her as she stumbled, fell backward and sat upright in water that rose to her waist.

"Oh, sweetheart! I'm sorry. Are you hurt?" he asked, grasping her hand to help her up.

"No, but..." With her other hand she tried to squeeze the water from her pullover. "Oh, I'm all wet!"

"That'll teach you to run from me!" He laughed. But the laughter was checked by a quick intake of breath as he stared down at her. Her hair had long since loosened from the ribbon tied at her neck and fell in disarray about her flushed face, and there was a smudge of paint on her cheek. She looked like a grubby, disheveled tomboy, and he had never desired a woman so much in his life. His hand tightening on hers, he drew her close, wrapping her in his arms. Kissing her hair with wild abandon. Kissing her temple, her eyelids. Capturing her mouth in long, lingering possession. Feeling her lips soft and yielding beneath his.

"Oh, Cicely. Cicely," he murmured, burying his face in the pulsating hollow at the base of her throat. Her skin was soft and warm from the sun, and her sweet fragrance mingled with the smell of water and wet earth. Almost involuntarily his hand slipped under her pullover to examine the satiny contours of her slender waist, to press the small mound of her breast. She gave a muted gasp and pressed closer, her arms stealing around him, her body molding itself so close that the water from her clothes soaked into his, evoking the curiously exciting sensation that she was melting into him.

He quivered with a passionate hunger and heard himself groan. In one swift movement he lifted her in his arms and started toward the beach. Her cry of protest stopped him.

"No!" It came out in a whisper muffled against his chest. And it was in direct contrast to the rapturous response of her body, which trembled in yielding surrender, as she pressed even closer. Her arms tightened around his neck and her fingers tangled convulsively in his hair.

"No?" he questioned, shifting her slight weight in his arms, and bending his head to look into her face.

She did not repeat the denial, and her wide blue eyes stared up at him helplessly, betraying a passion beyond her control. But he saw the doubt, the apprehension. And an appeal that touched him more than his own throbbing urgency. This was Cicely. This was not a casual affair to be impulsively consummated on a deserted beach. He must give her time to know that. Later, when he could trust himself to speak calmly and rationally, they would talk. Now it was all he could do to release her.

Slowly, reluctantly, he allowed her to stand, heard the little splash of water as her feet touched the riverbed. He could not resist holding her for a long moment and kissing her lightly before letting her go. Then, fighting to keep his control, he turned and walked down the beach, away from her.

Cicely felt relief as her feet touched the ground. Relief and overwhelming disappointment. It was almost as if she had been abandoned. Such wild delightful sensations had surged through her veins. She had experienced an erotic longing so intense that it had startled her, and she had struggled to break free.

But she hadn't wanted to be free! Even now, she was consumed by that compelling sweeping pull of her whole being, as if he were still holding her, touching her. Instead, he was several feet away, walking down the beach, hands in his pockets, kicking at the sand, as calm and relaxed as if he hadn't just kissed the life out of her two minutes before.

Was it her fault? Had she reacted so childishly that... Or been too eager? Too naive and inexperienced?

Both ashamed and appalled by such unfamiliar thoughts, Cicely tried to steady her wobbly knees. Tried to think. The stones. She wanted to take some home to copy the rich colors. She bent to the task, feeling the sun hot and comforting on her back as she determinedly splashed through the water, collecting and discarding. But her mind was in such turmoil that she could hardly discern the color of one stone from another. She soon gave it up and went back to drop the few she had gathered into her bag.

She sat on the blanket, her feet stretched out before her, unable to erase the feeling of being rejected. Abandoned. Just for a moment, she'd thought that he, too, had been consumed by the rapture that had swept through her. A rapture so new and strange... But perhaps not new to him. She thought of the women who always crowded around him at the tennis courts. She remembered the way he always smiled and listened to them, the gentle way he flirted with them. Sophisticated, knowing women. Women who knew how to please.

Maybe he doesn't want you to get the wrong idea, Cicely Roberts.

"Cicely, we need to talk."

She jerked her head up to see him standing before her. He bent down, resting on his heels, and brushed a little sand from her toe. "There are things you need to know about me."

"Oh, no!" It was not so much a reply to what he'd said as an involuntary gasp of pure pleasure. For his hand had cupped her foot, and his thumb was gently stroking. Suddenly the wild sweet sensations were beginning all over again. Then, as if sensing the powerful surge of emotion he was evoking, he released her foot and sat down beside her.

"No?" he asked. "Don't you want to know all about me?"

She shook her head. She just wanted him to kiss her, to hold her.

"My sister... Lisa told me that you—"

She put her finger to his mouth. He was going to talk about the check. Tell her about things that didn't matter.

Nothing mattered. Nothing but the inescapable intuitive feeling that there could be only one Mark Dolan in her life.

"Cicely, I want you to think," he said, moving her hand away from his mouth, kissing the palm. "Not just about this moment, but . . . but . . ." His breath caught as she held her fingers against his lips once again. She brushed her hand across his face, touching the crease in his cheek, pulling gently at his ear.

"Oh, Cicely, you're driving me crazy," he cried as he gathered her in his arms and guided her to lie beside him on the blanket. Electric swirls of pleasure spun through her as his mouth closed on hers, and she felt his hands warm on her bare back pressing her close.

"Oh, Mark," she moaned, winding her arms around his neck, thrusting her fingers into his hair. Her body strained toward his in an agony of wanting.

Then slowly he pulled away. He raised himself on one elbow and looked down at her. "Cicely, love, we need to come to some understanding. I want to tell you that—" But his lips were only a whisper away. And she had to lift her head only slightly to silence him with her mouth, slowly and enticingly. She felt him respond and sensed his desire, before he gave a long sigh and abruptly stood up.

"Come on," he said. "We're going home."

But this time she didn't feel abandoned. Only very frustrated. For she had seen her own passion mirrored in his eyes. She knew that he wanted her as much as she wanted him. It gave her a heady feeling. She felt happy and secure in that knowledge and laughed up at him. "In all the romances that Alicia reads," she teased, "it's the woman who kisses and runs away."

"You're shameless," he said with a short laugh, catching her hands and pulling her up. "But we're going home. Get your things together." Still, as she turned away, he drew her back and held her close for a long moment. He kissed her lightly, teasing her parted lips with his tongue. "I promise you, love, it won't always end this way. After we talk."

They didn't talk on the way home, for Cicely, engulfed in a delicious, happy languor, fell asleep against his shoulder. When they reached the house, he shook her gently, waking her. She looked up to see Daphne running down the walk.

"Oh, Cicely, I've been waiting and waiting. I didn't know how to get hold of you. Alicia...she's at the hospital. I had to call Emergency."

CHAPTER THIRTEEN

IT HURT HIM to see Cicely's distress. For a moment she just stood there on the sidewalk, her hand over her mouth, almost petrified. Then she became frantic, searching in the tote bag for her keys, throwing her precious drawings about and muttering incoherently.

"I've got to get to the hospital. I shouldn't have left her. She wanted me to stay. I was so impatient with her. Dear God...please. I didn't mean it. Oh...please."

She paid little attention to the teenager, who tried to tell her, "I think she's all right now. I called the hospital a little while ago. The nurse said she was breathing okay now. Cicely, I'm sorry. She kept choking and gasping. And I was so scared. I just called Emergency."

Mark realized he had to take charge. "Cicely," he said firmly, grasping her by the shoulders. "I'll drive you to the hospital. But you can't go looking like this. Go up and make yourself presentable and—"

"No! I'm going. And you needn't bother." She tried to break away, but he continued to hold her.

"It'll upset your mother to see you all disheveled." There, that got her attention. He spoke in a slow, clear voice. "Alicia is in the hospital. She's receiving the very best care. Now, you go up and get properly dressed and I'll drive you there. You don't want her to see how distressed you are."

"All right." Cicely yielded to his coaxing, turned and ran up the walk and into the house.

"I didn't know what else to do," the girl told Mark. "I know about the breathing machine but I just didn't want to take any chances."

"You did exactly right." He picked up the sketches that had fallen to the sidewalk, tried to put them in order and handed them to her. "Take these up to Cicely's workshop, please, where she can find them later. Then you can run along. I'll drive Cicely to the hospital. And don't worry. You did exactly right, and I'm sure Alicia's going to be fine."

"Yes," she said. "I tried to tell Cicely. You see, it all happened about one o'clock. I stayed here to wait for Cicely. But I called the hospital about four, and they said Alicia had made a dramatic recovery."

"Good." Yes, that wasn't surprising. Patients like Alicia often made a "dramatic recovery" once all attention was centered on them.

In a few minutes Cicely came down, a little pale, but looking quite lovely in a turquoise shift and matching flat sandals. He would not add to her very genuine distress. So, beyond reminding her of Daphne's assurances that Alicia had recovered, they rode in silence to the hospital. There he waited in a small anteroom while she went in to see her mother.

Cicely's heart pounded, and she took several deep breaths before opening the door of Room 302A. She moved quietly, so as not to disturb her mother.

But Alicia wasn't asleep. She was sitting up in bed, looking rested and refreshed, completely absorbed in *Dallas*, which was being aired on the television set suspended from the opposite wall. Cicely felt immensely relieved. But her apprehensions returned the minute Alicia saw her. The beautiful face puckered, the eyes filled with tears, and Alicia's body trembled.

"Oh, Cicely," she quavered, "It was horrible. Just horrible!"

"Now, now." Cicely rushed to put her arms around her mother. "It's all over. Don't get yourself upset again."

"But it was awful! Awful! And you weren't there. You don't know. You weren't there."

And I should have been, Cicely thought, as she cradled her mother, rubbing her back and trying to soothe her. *She told me this morning she wasn't feeling well, and I just went off and left her. Enjoying myself.* It had been like a holiday. The sketching, the painting. And . . . and other things. She felt herself blush as she remembered. She should have called home at lunchtime, when they were at the hamburger stand. She should have come home earlier. But the truth was that not once, not once during that whole long day, had she thought of her mother. How could she have been so neglectful?

She stayed with Alicia for a long time, hearing in infinite detail how frightened she'd been when she couldn't breathe properly.

"And that girl just panicked, didn't know what to do. And then those perfect strangers put me in an ambulance and brought me here. And nobody knew where you were!"

"Well, you should stop talking about it. You're only upsetting yourself. Get your mind on something else. Look, isn't that J.R.?"

"Oh, that horrible man!" Instantly diverted, Alicia again focused on the television. "Oh, I hope Sue Ellen won't take him back this time!"

"I must tell Mark not to wait," Cicely said, when she saw her mother engrossed in the program. "I'll be back."

"You're not going to leave me!"

"Just for a moment. I'll be right back."

"And you'll stay with me tonight? I don't want to be in this place by myself."

"Of course," Cicely assured her. "I just want to tell Mark so he can leave."

She found Mark still sitting in the anteroom, thumbing through a magazine. "How is she?"

"All right now, I think. Just a little nervous and upset."

"Did you talk to her doctor?"

"Yes. I phoned, back at the house. He keeps calling it stress. He said something must have upset her and... Oh, Mark, I think it was all my fault. She told me she wasn't feeling well this morning and she begged me to stay and I... well, I was feeling such pressure to get those fabric designs done. She kept asking me to stay with her, and I..." Cicely bit her lip. "Well, I got kind of impatient and irritated. I fobbed her off, told her I... we'd spend some time together this evening. Then I went off to do what I wanted to do!"

"About time," he muttered.

"What?" She glanced up, not sure she'd heard him correctly.

"Nothing. You were telling me what the doctor said."

"Oh, he seems to think she's all right now. Says he would have released her immediately, but I wasn't home."

"Good. Are we taking her home now?"

"Oh, no. We thought we'd just let her rest here overnight, since he's already admitted her. I'm going to stay with her."

"Why?"

"Well, she doesn't like to be alone."

"Alone? Cicely, this is a hospital." He sounded so exasperated that she started. "It's full of doctors, nurses, interns, aides—plenty of people to jump any time she pushes that little button."

"I know." She gave him a tentative, placating smile. "It's just that she feels better when I'm with her."

"I'll bet. What about you?"

"Me?" she asked, a little puzzled. "I—I'm fine."

He seemed about to say something, then changed his mind and gave a resigned shrug. "All right. Stay if you must. But let's get you something to eat."

"Oh, I'm not hungry. When she falls asleep—"

"When she falls asleep, the cafeteria will be closed, and you'll be at the mercy of those bloody vending machines. It's almost eight, and you've had nothing since that hamburger this afternoon. You're going to eat now."

"But I promised her I'd be right back."

"She'll survive." He put a commanding hand on her waist and led her to the elevator.

He couldn't really understand about Alicia, Cicely thought. The few times he'd seen her, she was at her best—on Thursday nights. She tried to make him understand as they descended to the cafeteria. Telling him how close Alicia had been to her husband, and how distraught at his death. Telling him about the battery of allergy tests she had endured, which had brought no definite results. And the frightening asthma attacks.

Mark said nothing. When she looked at him, she saw his mouth tighten as if he was annoyed.

The cafeteria was almost deserted, and the people behind the counter were clearing up. But the vegetable soup was still hot, so they each got a bowl and a sandwich. They took their trays to a corner table. The food was good, but Cicely barely tasted the soup and managed only a few bites of her sandwich. She felt so weary. It seemed that all of a sudden the whole day had become too much for her. The ramble through the hills . . . Mark . . . the anxiety about her mother. She hadn't realized it until she sat down, but she was simply too tired to eat.

"Why don't you let me take you home?" he asked gently.

"Oh, no. I couldn't leave Alicia."

"I know you're concerned." He hesitated. "But don't you think you're a little overconcerned, Cicely?"

"I can't help it. Lately these asthma attacks seem to have increased in frequency, and they're getting more severe. And it frightens me."

"I know. And you want to help her." He reached over to touch her hand. "But there *is* such a thing as helping too much. People who have asthma—or any other illness, for that matter—have to help cure themselves."

"What are you talking about?" she asked, drawing her hand away. "People can't just cure themselves."

"All right, all right. Of course, Alicia needs medical help and she needs your support." He frowned. "But sometimes just focusing away from the illness and getting involved in something else will work wonders for the patient."

"I know that. That's why I encourage her with the bridge games."

"Encourage her! You manage the whole thing. You set it up, you prepare the food, you—"

"And what's wrong with that?" she demanded, beginning to feel a little irritated.

"I'm just trying to tell you that you don't give her a chance to do anything for herself. You do everything for her. And, anyway, I didn't mean bridge. I mean something substantial. Like a job!"

"A job? Alicia has never worked a day in her life. And in her condition she couldn't possibly handle a job."

"You don't know what she can handle! Why don't you give her a chance to make up her own mind? You try to dictate her every move."

"And you try to dictate mine!" She threw down her spoon. "Ever since you met me, Mark Dolan, you've tried to manipulate me. You and your 'do what you like' philosophy. Do this. Do that. Send out your sketches and—"

He held up his hand. "You're missing my point."

"No. That is your point. You manipulated me into sending my sketches and... Oh, wipe that silly grin off your face!

All right, I'm glad I sent them. But I did it because I wanted to. Not because you urged me. And I certainly will not allow you to tell me what I should or should not do for my mother. This morning..." She broke off. She should never have left when Alicia wasn't feeling well.

"Ah, yes. This morning. She didn't want you to go and you left anyway. And now you feel guilty."

"That's ridiculous! Why should I feel guilty about my own mother?"

"Because you feel that whatever you do is not enough."

"Oh, you've got it all figured out, haven't you? You and your sidewalk psychology. Trying to talk like a shrink. Well, I think you're talking rubbish. And I'm not listening to another word. I'm going upstairs to stay with my mother like I should have stayed with her this morning."

"This morning again! Don't you ever listen to yourself? Sit down!" He took her wrist in such a firm grip that she was forced back into the chair from which she had started to rise. "Can't you perceive the patterns in your own life?" Shaking his head, he released her wrist. "Since I'm a shrink, as you so elegantly term it, that's—"

"Wait a minute. What did you say?"

"I said I'm a shrink. As in psychiatrist. And what I want you to know is—"

"Just be quiet a minute." Briefly the shock of the surprise held her anger in check. "Are you telling me that you really are an honest-to-goodness psychiatrist?"

"With all the credentials. And if you were paying one hundred and fifty dollars an hour for my advice, you'd bloody well take it!"

"Then what's your problem? Why aren't you practicing?"

"I am. That is, I do."

"No, you're not. You're running around doing nothing. Acting as if you didn't have a care in the world and making me think you were broke and—"

"I can't help what you assumed. I told you I was writing a book. I am. It's a book telling people how to live."

"Meanwhile practicing your theories on everyone you meet."

"What do you mean by that?"

"I mean the way you've tried to manipulate me ever since you've known me. Telling me I should do this or that. And you seem intent on building a wall between my mother and me. First, you said I didn't want to get rid of my glasses because I didn't want to compete with her. And now I'm to feel guilty because she needs me!"

"Oh, listen, Cicely—"

"No. You listen. I don't buy your analysis, Dr. Mark Dolan. So you can just take your advice right back to all those people who are paying all that money for it. Because I don't need it." She got up quickly and walked out.

Mark didn't try to stop her. He just stared after her in helpless frustration.

He remained there, sitting alone at the table, for some time, chin resting on his hand. Then he stacked their dishes and carried them to the conveyor. It was time to pay Alicia a visit.

CHAPTER FOURTEEN

A *psychiatrist*? Could that be true?

Of course it's true. He acts like one. Talks like one. Sitting back like some almighty I-know-just-what-you-need counselor! Observing. Commenting. Judging!

Oh, yes, he's a psychiatrist all right. Looking for a "pattern" behind every word I speak, every breath I take. Alicia's supposed to cure herself, is she—with all that choking and gasping. And, of course, there's something wrong with me just because I care about my mother!

Well, if you think I'm buying one bit of that psychiatric mumbo jumbo, Dr. Mark Dolan, you've got another think coming! I have no intention of neglecting my mother just because you think I should. And if I were in need of advice about how to run my own life, I certainly wouldn't seek it from someone who doesn't know how to run his own. Why all the secrecy about your profession? Why don't you take care of your own guilt feelings and leave mine alone!

Not that I feel guilty about taking care of my own mother. As a matter of fact, I plan to take better care of her. I've been too interested in my own career lately, and I've been neglecting Alicia.

So CICELY DECIDED to curtail her New York trips, and she applied to an agency for a housekeeper. She would reschedule her working hours to spend more time with Alicia and she resolved not to be distracted by... anybody!

That resolve almost melted when, two days after she brought Alicia home from the hospital, Cicely opened the door to Mark. And to the magnetic appeal his presence always held for her. That smile. Those eyes that regarded her so lovingly. So...analytically!

"Oh, hello, Mark." She managed to keep her voice icily polite. "It's good to see you. But I'm afraid this is bad timing. I'm very busy."

"Yes, I thought you might be. I really came to see Alicia." He stepped inside and bent toward her, speaking in a concerned whisper. "How is she?"

"Oh, you!" she sputtered, then said, "Very well. Thank you. Goodbye."

"But I thought I might visit her for a while. I—"

"No!" Cicely, conscious that her mother was in the nearby living room, lowered her own voice. "I know what you think of my mother. And I will not have you upsetting her!"

"Now would I do that?" His tone matched hers as he continued in a quiet, conspiratorial whisper. "You told me that any stress upsets her, and—"

"Look. Will you just leave! Kindly. And quietly."

"Oh, Cicely, you're just angry about what I said the other night. I'm afraid I was quite rash. And quite wrong. I realized later that, of course, you know your mother better than I do, and—"

"Cicely, honey, who is that?" Alicia called.

Before Cicely could speak, Mark replied, "It's Mark, Alicia. I came to check on you. How are you feeling?"

"Oh, Mark! Dear boy, do come in and see your roses. It was so sweet of you to send them. They really cheered me up."

Mark walked right past Cicely, giving her a look of such smug innocence that she fumed. Anxiously she followed him into the living room, and heard him speaking solicitously to

Alicia. "It's so good to see you, Alicia. You're looking lovely as usual. And after that awful bout you had the other day."

"Oh, well, I try not to let it get me down. Oh, Mark, it's so fortunate that you dropped by. I wanted to ask you—can you substitute tomorrow night? Leonard has another meeting."

"Yes, I'd be glad to. I've missed the group. And about bridge, Alicia, did you read the column in today's *Bee*?"

"Of course. That's the first thing I read every morning."

"Well, would you mind explaining something to me? I didn't quite understand North's bid." He looked up at Cicely. "Oh, Cicely, don't let us keep you. I know how busy you are. I'm just going to visit a while with Alicia."

"Oh, well, I..." Cicely stood for a moment, feeling awkward and uncertain. And annoyed. What exactly was he up to?

"But that was the only bid North could possibly make. Don't you see?" Alicia picked up the paper and turned to the bridge column. "His hand holds four spades and—"

"Wait," Mark interrupted. "Let me get a deck of cards. Aren't they here?" He walked over to the side table and secured one. "Yes. Let's lay the cards out and you can show me." They bent over the cards, completely ignoring her, and Cicely felt like a fifth wheel. Finally she gave a shrug and left them. If all they were going to talk about was bridge, she might as well get back to work.

Mark did manage to play bridge with the group the next night, and made three more "home calls" on Alicia during the week. The first two times he didn't see Cicely at all. The door was opened by a stout, matronly woman, whom Alicia introduced as Mrs. McGinnis, their new housekeeper.

Good, he thought. At last Cicely was realizing that she didn't have to do everything herself. But it had its bad effects. It meant he wasn't seeing Cicely, and five days without seeing her was a bit too long. Especially when they'd parted on such bad terms. Maybe, he thought, as he left home to make his third call on Alicia, he could persuade Cicely to go out for dinner. If he managed to catch sight of her.

But this time he was lucky. This time the door was opened by Cicely. His Cicely. Tousled hair. Tattered pullover. Bare feet. She said nothing, but her look told him she was as glad to see him as he was to see her.

"Something new has been added," he said, touching the paint splotches on her pullover.

"Yes." She glanced down at the smudges, then back at him. "I've been trying to match the colors of the rocks. Not the rock formation itself, but just the way those rich colors blend and flow into one another. Almost like a river." Her voice trailed off as their eyes met, and memory, like a melody, sang between them. That long day together. The flowers. The stones in the water. That moment on the beach.

"Cicely. Cicely." His hand reached out to cup her chin.

There was a burst of laughter from the living room, and she drew back as if recalled to other things. Other people.

"Come in. Mr. Spencer's here and I'd like you to meet him."

He followed her into the living room, where Alicia sat with—yes, indeed—the great Brick Spencer himself. He had all the appearance of a mover and a shaker. And, Mark thought, the rugged handsome looks that appealed to most women.

"I think we've met before," Spencer said to him. "You're the family friend who detained Cicely that evening she dined with me in Sacramento."

"Yes. How do you do?" Mark recalled every aspect of that evening. He remembered with painful clarity how awe-struck Cicely had been in this man's presence.

After some small talk, Mark learned that Spencer had just spent a week in Hawaii and had decided, on the spur of the moment, to stop off in California.

"To have a visit with my new partner," Spencer said, smiling at Cicely. "And there's no doubt that I caught her hard at work."

And no doubt that the picture of Cicely at work appeals to you, Mark fumed, resenting the appreciative gleam in Spencer's eyes as his gaze traveled over Cicely.

"And now, my dear—" Spencer stood and spoke directly to Cicely "—aren't you going to show me where you produce all those wonderful creations?"

"Oh, yes. Please excuse us." Cicely gave Mark a casual glance, then turned to Spencer. "Come this way."

Mark, his eyes on Cicely's bare feet, watched them depart. He was shocked by the towering rage that shook him. He'd always prided himself on the control he had over his emotions. And he was certainly no chauvinist. He was proud of Cicely's career. Of course, she had to confer with her associates occasionally; of course, he wasn't jealous! But no other man had a right to look at Cicely in the well...disheveled state she was always in while she worked. And no other man had the right to share that sparkle of enthusiasm. He could see her now, up there in that cluttered workshop, her hair falling around her face, looking vibrantly alive as she talked about the flow of muted colors. Or how she was going to drape this or that. And he could see Spencer watching her. He wanted to go upstairs, throw Cicely over his shoulder and—

"Mark, you're not listening to me."

Dimly he became aware that Alicia was trying to get his attention. It wouldn't work anyway. Even if he resorted to such caveman tactics, Cicely would soon turn back to "see about Alicia."

First things first, he told himself grimly. Somehow, he had to instill some measure of independence in Alicia. But this was proving to be an almost insurmountable task.

"If I could just get her involved or even interested in something productive. Something that would challenge her," he said to Richard, as they stood together on the back lawn the next afternoon.

"I want to engender some sense of responsibility in my boys," Richard mused, regarding the freshly cut grass. "And I don't think it's too much to ask a twelve-year-old boy to walk behind a power-driven mower."

"But the only thing that interests her, besides herself, is bridge."

"On the other hand," Richard said, "the gardener wouldn't knock off the sprinkler heads. And if he did, he'd replace them. Oh, well, guess I'll have to do it myself," he said, bending down to pick up one of the heads.

"No, no, no," Mark insisted, brushing him aside. "Better let me do that. Can't afford to rough up your million-dollar hands. Besides, if you want to teach responsibility... Hey, you guys!" he called to the two boys who were tossing a basketball through a hoop on the garage door. "Whose turn to cut the lawn?"

"Mine," Denis answered. "I did it already."

"Then there's a little matter for you to attend to. Bring me a wrench from the garage." When the boy brought the wrench, Mark pointed to the sprinkler head and said, "Your job isn't finished until you've repaired any damage you've done in the process."

"But I don't know how to fix a sprinkler head," Denis protested.

"So learn. Look here." Mark knelt to demonstrate.

"There's another one over there," Richard reminded them when they were finished.

"I'll do it. I know how. I can do it by myself," Denis cried. He fixed it and went back to the basketball game obviously very proud of himself.

"A bit of accomplishment is what engenders a sense of responsibility," Mark said to Richard, as they both sat on the patio. "Now what on earth could Alicia Roberts accomplish?"

"Don't bring me your problems," Richard picked up his newspaper. "I've got enough of my own. Ruth Carter's husband is being transferred and she's leaving us."

"I don't believe Alicia has ever accomplished anything in her life."

"She's been with us five years and she knows all the patients who come to our medical center."

"I don't think Alicia has ever felt responsible for anything or anybody."

"Best receptionist we've ever had. I don't know how we'll replace her."

"Receptionist? Replace her?" Mark sat up, his full attention now on what Richard was saying.

Richard put down his newspaper. "No, you don't. I draw the line at your prospective mother-in-law."

"But Alicia would make a perfect receptionist. She's beautiful, and charming and—"

"Charming? Beautiful? Can this be the same woman to whom you attributed such qualities as irresponsible...self-involved...lazy?"

"Which qualities in no way detract from her beauty and charm. Why, it would give your patients a lift just to look at her."

"Helpless? Dependent?"

"But don't you see? Once she's given some responsibility and begins to feel a sense of accomplishment, it would do wonders for her."

"We are not a charitable institution, Mark. Sorry."
Richard picked up his newspaper again.

"But really, if you've got to replace this woman—"

"No. I pride myself on competence in my employees. A woman who has no experience—"

"How much experience do you need to answer a telephone and point people to the right door?" Here, Mark perceived, was a golden opportunity. This was a job Alicia could handle. Here was something that would not only get her out of the house, but engender that needed feeling of self-worth and accomplishment. He increased his persuasions. By the time Lisa appeared on the terrace carrying a tray with three tall glasses of iced tea, Richard was reluctantly agreeing to give Alicia a try.

"Oh, Mark," Lisa said, "Crystal Morris called. She's trying to arrange a time for both of you to meet with your publisher in New York. To talk about the promotion campaign for your book. So don't forget to return her call."

"All right," Mark answered rather absently. Richard had agreed. Now if he could just persuade Alicia.

"And we came up with another idea," Lisa continued. "As soon as your final revisions are approved, Crystal thinks Richard and I should give a prepublication party. We'll make it very posh, black tie and all, so I can wear that beautiful lace dress you bought me, Mark. Don't you think that's a good idea, Richard?"

"I do, if it means he's finished that book and is going home to leave us in peace."

"Richard, you know you enjoy my brother." Lisa walked over to rumple her husband's hair.

"Your brother I can tolerate. It's his love life that gets to me. Too much thinking and plotting. Why can't he just pick up the girl and haul her off to England?"

"I thought of that, old chap. But I knew it wouldn't work." Mark grinned. "However, this plan might. Thanks, pal."

CICELY STARED at her mother, who was taking one dress after another from her closet. "Alicia, what are you doing?"

"I'm trying to decide what to wear to work tomorrow."

"Work? What are you talking about?"

"I knew you'd be surprised." Alicia's smile, bright and rather smug, showed that she was pleased at putting something over on Cicely. "I've got a job."

"Alicia, you've never worked in your life. What on earth are you talking about? Who would...I mean, where would you get a job?"

"What do you think of this, dear?" Alicia held a lightweight knit of pale green under her chin and studied her image in the mirror. "I think it does something for my eyes. Mark says it's important that I look my best."

"Mark?" Cicely breathed a little faster as a suspicion dawned. "What does he have to do with this?"

"Oh, I'm really doing him a favor. You see, his cousin— no, I think it's his uncle...that eye doctor who did your surgery, Cicely. Did you know he was a relative of Mark's? And you didn't tell me he was so handsome and so nice. He hired me on the spot."

Cicely stood in stupefied silence as Alicia rattled on. "What's his name—Hardy? No, Hartley, I think. Anyway, Mark said he was just going crazy because his receptionist had quit. It was so difficult to find just the right person to replace her, because that position is so special, you know. Mark said they need someone who is attractive and cheerful and charming and knows just how to deal with people. And Mark said he immediately thought of me." Alicia waved a hand. "So I start tomorrow."

"But Alicia, you've never worked! And you don't need to. We don't need the money."

"I know, dear. I told you. I'm doing Mark a favor. He says his cousin has been so nice to him. And, really, you know, Mark has been nice to us, filling in at bridge and all. I couldn't refuse him. Maybe I should wear this blue. What do you think?"

"Wait, Alicia. Come here and sit down and let's talk this over." Cicely pulled her mother to sit on the chaise and knelt before her. "Now, I'm not sure it's a good thing for you to go to work. I know you've been feeling better, but you remember what Dr. Davison said about stress. And with your allergies—"

"But that's just it. Mark said—"

"Oh, my goodness!" Cicely stood to run a hand distractedly through her hair. If she says "Mark said" just one more time!

"What's the matter, dear?"

"Nothing," Cicely said through clenched teeth. "Go on. What did Mark say?"

"That this would be the ideal place for me to work. You see, it's a medical complex. There are six...no, let me think. Maybe there are eight or nine doctors. I'm not sure about that. But I do know there's a nose and throat man. And an allergy specialist. Mark says I would be safer there than at home."

"And just where is this marvelous safer-than-home place?"

"It's the Hardy...or is it Harkness Medical Center. And it's in Fair Oaks. And Mrs. McGinnis is going to drive me back and forth. Mark said it was clever of you to hire a housekeeper who can drive. So you see everything is settled. Maybe this blue dress will be better for the first day. What do you think, dear?"

"CICELY, HOW NICE of you to call." Mark's husky voice was cheerful when she got him on the phone. "I've been wanting to talk with you."

"I suppose that's why you've been sneaking around behind my back trying to persuade my—"

"Sneaking? Why, I've come to your front door each time I visited. And hoping each time to catch a glimpse of your beautiful face."

"Sneaking! And persuading my mother to take a job when... Oh, Mark, how could you? Alicia's never worked a day in her life. And now, when she's not well..."

"Take it easy, Cicely. Having a job will be the best thing that can happen to your mother. She needs to know that she can take care of herself."

"She does not need the stress. And I am perfectly capable of taking care of her."

"Ah, love... Don't you see? She needs to take some responsibility, get her mind on something besides herself, feel that she—"

"Mark, please save your psychiatry for your paying customers. I am not one of them. And neither is my mother!"

"But, Cicely, I do have a check, signed by you, in the amount of five hundred dollars."

"You know what that check is for. It's certainly not for psychiatric treatment! And my mother is not a guinea pig. So why don't you just leave her alone?"

"Ah, Cicely. I care about your mother. I really do. And I care for you. I'm only doing what I think is best—"

"There you go again! What *you* think is best! I warn you, Mark Dolan, if you don't leave my mother alone, I'm going to sue you for malpractice!"

"But if she's not my patient and—"

"For undue persuasion and practicing on someone who didn't request it, then! There must be some law that protects innocent citizens against meddling psychiatrists."

"Ah, now, Cicely..." His low chuckle was so irritating that she slammed down the phone. He was impossible.

If Alicia becomes ill, if anything at all happens to her, I will not be responsible for what I might do to you. So just watch out, Mark Dolan!

CHAPTER FIFTEEN

TWO WEEKS LATER, Cicely sat at the breakfast table and looked across at her mother. Every day she'd been expecting and—she had to admit—searching for signs of stress. There were none. In fact, she'd never seen Alicia so animated.

"There are three of us who always go out to lunch together," Alicia was saying. "Today we're going back to the Coffee Tree. That's where we took Ruth last week. It's a very elegant place."

"Well, you're certainly dressed for it," Cicely said, thinking how smart her mother looked in the lavender slacks and matching sweater. "I love that color on you."

"Thank you, dear. I wore pink the day we went there with Ruth. She's the one I'm replacing, you know, and she's been so nice, showing me everything, that I got her this lovely gift from that jewelry store in the center. Her husband's in the service and she has this charm bracelet with charms from every place she's been. So that's what I got her—a bear, representing California, you know."

"Oh, that was thoughtful. I know she liked it."

"Yes, she did. Only when she opened it, Louella—that's Dr. Martin's nurse—or Dr. Miller's. Anyway, she said it was a koala bear. But Ruth said a bear's a bear. And that's what I thought, too. And it doesn't matter because the koala bear is the symbol for Australia...and that's where they are going...or is that where they were stationed before they came here?'' Alicia took a mouthful of melon and pondered this question.

"I've been meaning to tell you," Cicely said, wondering if this was a good time. "I've got to go back to New York tomorrow."

"That's nice, dear. Mrs. McGinnis and I will arrange for the bridge. We're going to have a speaker."

Cicely felt a surge of relief. Her mother didn't seem to mind at all about her going away. And this change had occurred in just two weeks. Was Alicia already feeling more independent? Mark had said this was the best thing that could happen to her mother. And Cicely had said... *Oh, why do I get so angry with him?*

Because he's so bossy and dictatorial! And right?

"Thank you, Mrs. McGinnis," Cicely said, as the housekeeper removed the fruit plates and served the bacon and eggs. Then she handed a slip of paper to Cicely.

"Pardon me," she said. "But I wanted you to check this grocery list. Is this all we need? I thought I might stop by the market after I take Mrs. Roberts to work."

"Oh, you don't need to take me," Alicia cried. "Stephen is picking me up."

"Stephen?" Cicely asked, as both women stared at Alicia.

"Stephen Poindexter. That's his name. But Cicely, you'll never guess who he really is!"

"No, I won't," Cicely said. She'd never met the man. But she was seeing something in her mother's eyes she hadn't seen for a long time.

"Oh, it was the funniest thing. When he came in the other day, I sent him to the wrong suite. Because there was another man, a Mr. Stephens, who was supposed to come in for contacts. Dr. Hardy was a bit upset, but Dexter—that's what he prefers to be called—just laughed. He said he couldn't understand why they were testing his eyes for al-

lergies . . . because that's what he has, you see. So when he
came out, I told him about the relaxation technique Mark
showed me. When you feel you're going to have trouble
breathing, you just close your eyes, and sit calmly and say
this chant to yourself. It really works. Only I've never used
it but once because—well, I just haven't felt ill since I started
working. I think the air over there is better for me.''

Mark had helped. He really did care.

''And he said he'd try it. Then he told me who he really
is. Cicely would you believe this? He's Dexter Diamond.''

''Oh. But . . . who's Dexter Diamond?''

''Really, Cicely. His column is in the paper every morning. The bridge column. He said he didn't want to use his
real name. And he wanted to use a name that related to
cards. So he settled on Diamond. And the first name—
Dexter, from Poindexter. Do you see? Isn't he clever? Well,
and then we got to talking about his column, because I really
disagreed with what he said that day and . . . Oh, there he is
now. I must go. No, wait. Cicely, you let him in while I
freshen my lipstick.''

Cicely opened the door to a distinguished-looking man,
who was just a little taller than herself. His dark hair was
graying at the temples, and he wore a pair of wire-rimmed
glasses.

''Good morning,'' he said. ''You must be Cicely.''

''Yes. Do come in. Would you like a cup of coffee?''

Dexter declined the coffee, saying he didn't want to make
Alicia late for work. Cicely watched them as they went down
the walk, Alicia smiling up at him and talking in that animated way. It was a miracle, she thought, the way Alicia had
changed. She was more like her old self, the way she was
before Dad died.

I'm going to tell Mark that he was right. Would he want
to talk with her, though? During that first week of Alicia's
employment, Mark had called twice and invited Cicely to

dinner. But she was angry and had turned him down. And let's face it, Cicely. You were obnoxious!

But he hadn't seemed to mind. All he'd said was "just wait and see." Still, there hadn't been any word from him during the past several days, and she was a little apprehensive. Maybe...maybe he was angry.

No. Mark was never really angry. Every time they'd had a conflict, he had returned almost as if they'd never said such shocking words to each other. Almost as if they'd parted friends. He would look at her with that teasing smile; he'd say something to delight her or make her laugh. She felt a warm glow steal through her at the memory. Mark always understood, she told herself, and he never held grudges.

Cicely went to the telephone and dialed, eagerly anticipating that husky British voice. She would start talking on a teasing note. She'd say, "I won't sue you after all. You were right."

"ALL RIGHT. ALL RIGHT. Maybe I was wrong," Mark said, as he tossed his bag into the back seat of Richard's car, then slid in beside him. "But don't do anything rash. When I get back from New York—"

"Damn right, you were wrong! And I can't wait for you to get back." Richard drove the car out of the driveway, and headed for the airport. "I've got to do something now. The place has been a shambles since Ruth left."

"In one week?"

"In one week. You may not realize it, pal, but it does take some degree of acumen to press the right buttons on the telephone and point people to the right door. And your Alicia Roberts...well, take this for example. She called in a lab report the other day that scared the devil out of me."

"Oh?"

"The thing was, I had a routine checkup the day before. And when she called to give me the blood report from the lab, I thought...well, let me tell you, it gave me night-mares. Was I relieved when I learned it was a mistake. The report was for endocrinology and it was for a man named Hardy. Poor guy.'' Richard sighed as he pulled out to pass a truck.

"Oh, I see. Hardy—Hartfield. She mixed up the names.''

"She ought to at least know the patients from the doctors. I was worried all day. And then some guy named Poindex-ter came in and I tested him for contacts before I learned he was in to see Miller about allergies! And Miller was about to give an allergy test to a girl who was slated for dermatol-ogy.''

"I can see you have a problem.'' Mark rubbed his chin thoughtfully. This was a disaster; he thought he'd found the perfect place for Alicia, and his scheme *was* working. At least on Alicia. She had been positively beaming the day he dropped into the medical center to check on her. "I do think the job has been good for her.''

"For her, maybe. But not for us. No, Mark, she has to go. I'm already interviewing applicants.''

"Well, that's it,'' Mark said, brightening. "Hire some-body to do the work and I'll pay her. No, I'll pay Alicia and all she has to do is sit there and look pretty. She does that very well, doesn't she?''

"Oh, she does that. Very well. You ought to see her flashing that smile and apologizing oh so sweetly whenever she makes a mistake. That guy with the allergy problems, the one I tested for contacts. He's been hanging around Alicia's desk every day since. He can't be that ill!''

"Then that's it,'' Mark said again, as Richard pulled into the loading zone at the airport. "It won't cost you a thing. I'll pay Alicia just to be charming, and you can hire some-body to do the real work.''

"And what will I tell Alicia so she won't be sending peo-ple to the wrong doctor and—''

"Don't tell her anything. I'm sure you can hire someone smart enough to circumvent any mistakes Alicia might make." Mark reached into the back and got his suitcase. "And thanks for the lift, pal. See you in a few days. Cheers."

THE FIRST NIGHT Cicely was in New York, Spencer kissed her. It caught her so much by surprise that she didn't resist. At least not at first. And later, when she thought about it, she was glad that he had kissed her. Someone had said that there was something to be learned from every experience. Well, she had learned much from that kiss.

She had made the trip this time to take her fabric designs out to the mill and to choose the kind of cloth into which they'd be woven. George had set up the appointment, so she expected him to meet her at the airport. But when she arrived at Kennedy, it was Spencer who awaited her.

"I thought I'd drive you to the mill myself," he said, "and help you choose the fabric."

"Oh, that...that's kind of you." She refrained from telling him that she didn't want the help. Only she could choose the fabrics that would suit her designs. Still, it made the trip convenient, and she did enjoy his company.

It took two hours to reach the mill, which was located in upstate New York. The day was bright and sunny, with only a hint of chill in the air. Cicely found the beauty of the countryside breathtaking. "I've always heard that the fall colors in New England are spectacular," she told Spencer. "But that's also true of New York, I see."

"You'll find that New York has a lot to offer in all four seasons. Do you ski, Cicely?"

She said no, she didn't, and he said that was a pity. She should learn. He had a cabin in the Adirondacks; perhaps on one of her visits, she could go up and he'd give her lessons.

At the mill, to Cicely's great relief, he didn't try to help her choose the fabric. He just stood back and watched as she surveyed sample after sample and, to her delight, found just what she wanted. On the way back, they stopped at a country inn for dinner. They discussed her work, and she used a paper napkin to sketch some ideas she had in mind. He smiled at her enthusiasm.

"I think I've discovered your secret," he said. "You take so much joy in the creation that it comes through in the finished product. That's what makes your fashions so fresh and original."

"Thank you." Mark was right about that, too. *Do what makes you happy.*

"You and I make a good team, Cicely. I'm as enthusiastic about marketing your product as you are about creating it."

"Oh...yes." She'd phoned Mark several times before she left and received no answer. Suddenly she had an overwhelming desire to see him. To talk. To tell him he was right. When she got home tomorrow—

"...and wouldn't you like to come along?"

"I beg your pardon?" Embarrassed, she realized that Spencer had been talking and she hadn't heard any of it.

"The Orient. I'm making a trip there next month. I was suggesting you might come along and maybe pick up some new ideas."

"Oh, I think not. I have all I can manage, if I'm to be ready in time for the April showing."

"Oh, yes. That reminds me," he said, pausing to take a sip of wine. "We're meeting with Sue tomorrow to talk about that showing. She wants to discuss some office-to-party fashions."

"Tomorrow? But I'm leaving in the morning."

"That's impossible, my dear. Everything's already arranged. And the next day, we have another meeting with the graphic artist."

"Oh, I'm sorry. I didn't know." Cicely tried to hide her dismay and her vague suspicion that both these meetings were unnecessary. But she didn't want to seem uncooperative, and he'd been so nice about driving her out to the mill. So she said of course she would stay. By the time he took her back to the hotel suite, Cicely had lost much of her awe of Brick Spencer. He came in, fixed their after-dinner drinks and continued to entertain her with anecdotes about his dealings in world commerce.

"You do lead an interesting life," she said. "Such a variety of different experiences."

"Would you like to share some of them?"

"What?" Too late she realized her response had been abrupt, but she wasn't sure what he meant.

"If you came to Japan with me, I can show you all kinds of things, introduce you, take you places."

She put down her drink and stood up. "Oh, no, I don't think..." She didn't finish the sentence, for he, too, stood and cupped her face in his hands.

"Come with me, Cicely of California. We could have a great time together."

"No. Your business... I wouldn't like to interfere," she gasped.

"I told you. I never allow business to interfere with pleasure." And before she could say anything, she was in his arms and he was kissing her.

She was totally unprepared, and for a long moment remained passive and unresisting as she felt herself pressed close to a strong, muscular body. She breathed the odor of Scotch and a pungent after-shave and felt gentle hands caressing her and the pressure of demanding lips on hers. It was the kiss of an expert.

And it left her utterly cold.

She pushed her hands against his chest and turned her head away.

"Cicely, don't be afraid of me."

"It's not that. I—"

"All right, darling. I won't rush you." His fingers teased her hair. "Cicely, think about Japan, will you?"

"But I won't ... I mean ... yes, I'll think about it." She backed away from him. "But now it's late. And I'm rather tired."

"I'll go now, but we'll talk about it tomorrow."

"Yes. Good night."

When he went out, she closed the door and leaned against it. But her mind was far from the man who had just kissed her. Mark. Her instincts had been right. There could be only one man in her life. Mark Dolan. He was the only man whose kiss went beyond her lips.

The meeting with Sue wasn't scheduled until late afternoon the next day. So Cicely had the whole morning to amuse herself. She went shopping and bought a lovely pale lavender blouse for her mother and a dress for herself. A special dress.

She was a little nervous about seeing Spencer again. She wished she'd taken lessons from Debby—or Alicia—on how to discourage flirtatious men without offending them. She'd had no experience herself in dealing with such relationships and she couldn't always determine when another person was sincere or just being casually flirtatious. And she found it hard to rebuff either approach, hard to reject and risk wounding someone. Not only that, she really liked Spencer and wanted to do nothing that would disrupt their friendly business relationship.

Spencer's manner, when he called for her at the hotel, was appropriately businesslike and affectionately friendly. However, Cicely wasn't completely disarmed. He insisted that later in the evening he'd take her out to dinner, and she knew she'd have to deal with the usual "after-dinner drink."

After the meeting with Sue, Spencer had to stop by his office to return a few long-distance calls and consult with some associates. It was almost eight when they arrived at the Marriott. He'd decided they would dine at the restaurant on top as it afforded an excellent view of the city.

"It is beautiful!" Cicely gasped, dazzled by the myriad of lights shining from every window of the tall buildings, outlining the bridges and beaming from the vehicles in the lines of traffic that moved across them. The restaurant revolved, so she got a glimpse of the city from every direction.

Spencer smiled at her enthusiasm. "I thought you'd like it!" and to her discomfort, added, "There are so many things I'd like to show you."

It was after the waiter brought a dessert menu that Spencer mentioned the trip to Japan again. He discounted all her very diplomatic reasons for not accompanying him. Finally Cicely excused herself, and in an effort to collect her thoughts, retreated to the ladies' room.

There she dallied a few minutes, pondering the best way to decline. Perhaps honesty. "I don't want to go with you." No, that was too blunt. "I don't want to give you the wrong idea." Too presumptuous. Could she possibly say "I'm involved in a serious relationship and . . ." But she wasn't. Or was she?

That moment by the river, Mark had acted as if he felt the same way she did. But then he'd pushed her away. And later, they had argued. . . .

Oh, Mark, I wish I could see you now.

Two minutes later, she did. As she left the ladies' room, she almost bumped into him. For one shocked moment, she wondered if her desire had conjured him into being, but the touch of his hand on her arm, steadying her, convinced her he was really there.

"Cicely," he cried, and she was pleased at the look of joyous recognition on his face. "Can it be fate, our meeting at restaurants? It must be of some significance."

Cicely could not speak. She smiled up at him, thinking how handsome he looked in the dark blue suit, wishing she could tell him that—

She heard a woman cough and saw Mark turn politely.

"Oh, Crystal, you remember Cicely Roberts, don't you?"

"Oh, dear, I'm so bad at remembering names," Crystal answered in a puzzled tone and looking condescendingly at Cicely. "I just don't recall. Have we met?"

"Yes. At the tennis club in Sacramento," Cicely said, vividly recalling that this was the woman in the seductive bikini, the woman who had detained Mark so long that Sunday morning. "How do you do?" she managed, while wondering if all Crystal's garments were of that French cut. How else was it that the gold lamé dress she wore appeared even more provocatively revealing than the bikini?

"Can you join us, Cicely?" Mark asked eagerly. He looked around. "I mean you and your escort, of course."

"Thank you. But we were about to leave."

"Just for dessert and coffee, perhaps," he suggested, paying no attention to Crystal's "Really, Mark, you shouldn't keep her."

"No, thank you. It's been good to see both of you," Cicely said stiffly as she started to move away.

"Wait. Perhaps we can get together tomorrow. How long will you be here?" he asked.

"I'm leaving around noon," she answered, and before Mark could speak, Crystal broke in.

"Oh, that's too bad. Mark and I will be here for several days and it would have been good to see you again. But—" she gave a little wave "—c'est la vie!" She placed a possessive hand on his arm. "Darling, the waiter is ready to seat us. Do excuse us," she said to Cicely.

But Cicely was already hurrying away, unable to face Crystal's insincere smile. *Mark and I will be here for several days.*

Cicely felt chilled and numb, and she was breathing hard when she rejoined Spencer. But she pasted a bright smile on her face, determined not to let her agitation show.

"I'm sorry," she said. "I was detained."

"I saw. By your...er...family friend?"

"Yes." She looked at him, trying to decide what she detected in his voice. He only smiled.

"I ordered cheesecake for you. I remembered that you said you liked it."

"Yes." She hated cheesecake. But she'd said she liked it the evening they met and had ordered it to make more time to discuss the dress shop. She forced herself to take a forkful.

"Your friend...Dolan, is it?"

She nodded, willing herself not to look toward Mark's table.

"He must be a very good friend indeed."

"Not really." She had said that before, too. That same night. And it had been true then. But it wasn't true now. Or was it?

No, Mark was a good friend, whatever his relationship with Crystal Morris. The thought of what might be between those two gave her such a feeling of anguish that she bit her lower lip and blinked several times. But she told herself she had no right to be so angry. Or to cry.

Anyway, whatever the truth, things you said had a way of coming back to haunt you. It was better to be honest and direct. "Listen," she ventured. "About Japan—"

Spencer reached across to put his hand over hers. "Never mind about Japan. Believe it or not, I am rather perceptive. I can hear a no, even if you don't say it."

That evening he did not come in for an after-dinner drink.

CHAPTER SIXTEEN

WHEN CICELY RETURNED HOME, she found an invitation in her mail.

> Dr. and Mrs. Richard Hartfield request the pleasure of your company at a reception in honor of Mark Dolan, M.D., whose first book, *Life Is for Living,* is to be released by American Publishing Company, in March of next year.

So Mark had finished his book. His guide to living a happy life. Cicely felt a glow of pride, quickly replaced by a pang of regret. He would be going home now. Yet she wondered how much she'd see of him even if he were here, since he seemed to be otherwise occupied.

There was also an invitation for her mother. That was thoughtful of Mark. But, then, that was just the kind of gesture he would make.

Mark. Since she'd seen him that night in New York, Cicely had been trying hard to get him out of her mind...out of her heart. She couldn't. He seemed a part of everything she said or did, the very air she breathed. And in spite of everything, Cicely was warmed by his persistent, if invisible, presence—smiling approvingly as she worked over her designs. Teasing her gently. Touching her.

But he's not here with me! He was in New York with Crystal Morris. And the thought of Mark with another woman, smiling, teasing, touching *her*, engulfed Cicely in such a wave of despair that she felt sick.

Her spirits might have been bolstered, or at least sustained, had she been able to muster raging anger or bitter jealousy. But Cicely was diminished by a feeling of hopeless envy. For her old sense of inadequacy had returned. How could she ever expect to compete with women like Crystal Morris? Experienced, knowledgeable women. Mark had realized she was different. That was why, that day at Bear River, when she'd thrown herself at him, he had pushed her away. Gently and kindly. But definitely away.

CICELY DRESSED very carefully for Mark's party. All her own creations had to be reserved for the April showing, so she wore the dress she had purchased in New York. It was a red velvet sheath dress that molded softly to her figure and had a very low back. It would have been mini-length except for its flounce of silk fringe which began five inches above her knees and fell to midcalf. A daring dress, but Cicely was glad that it was daring. Glad that it was red. She needed the courage.

Alicia looked lovely in her favorite shade of pale lavender. Cicely was gratified to see her mother excited about a party; it reminded her of countless childhood evenings when she'd watched Alicia get dressed in a flutter of happy anticipation.

Dexter Diamond, Alicia's new friend, was to escort them, and he arrived exactly on time, looking very distinguished and correct in his black tuxedo.

As they drove toward the Hartfield home, Cicely, her hands clasped tightly together, sat in the back seat of Dexter's Cadillac, willing herself to be calm. She was going to be cheerful and casually friendly. "Congratulations, Mark," she'd say. "I'm looking forward to seeing your book in print."

Would she ever have the chance to really talk to him, to tell him, "You were right. And I appreciate what you did for Alicia"?

Well, she wouldn't be able to say anything personal to him tonight. Loads of people were going to be there. She'd just act friendly and— She caught her breath as she realized Dexter had stopped the car and was getting out to open the doors for her and Alicia. She felt a strong desire to shrink back into a corner and say, "I'm feeling a little faint. Why don't you two go on in and I'll wait here for a while."

"Thank you," she said, when Dexter helped her out. Oh, lord, she couldn't! She couldn't walk in there in front of all those people and see him with Crystal, standing right beside him, simpering up at him, clutching his arm. *And I can't bear it. I can't!*

"Oh yes, I thought there would be quite a crowd," she said in answer to Dexter, as they walked past the cars that lined the street and stood parked in the circular driveway. The house, a two-story mansion that seemed to be all glass and cedar siding, was set well back from the street. It was blazing with lights, and they could hear voices and laughter as they approached.

The door was opened by a maid who took their wraps. Then Lisa hurried forward to greet them. "Hello, Cicely. I'm so glad you're here."

Lisa was wearing *her* dress. Cicely couldn't believe it. The beige lace, with the rhinestones . . . the one she had labored on so long, the one Mark had admired. Lisa caught her look and stepped back, smiling impishly.

"Well, do I do it justice?"

"Oh, yes. It's perfect on you!" Cicely was lost in admiration of her own work, watching the graceful sway of the dress, as Lisa twirled to show it off.

"I'll fill you in later," Lisa whispered, then turned to greet the others. "You're Alicia, of course. How nice that you could come."

She led them into a large room filled with people and immediately began to make introductions. Cicely smiled at the people she met and fervently engaged in small talk with whoever happened to be standing near her. But she was conscious of only one person.

Mark, wonderfully handsome in his black-tie array, stood in a corner of the room opposite to Cicely's. He was surrounded by a host of admirers, and Cicely wasn't sure that he had even noticed her. Someone handed her a glass of champagne. A woman in blue velvet approached and spoke to Dexter. "You're Dexter Diamond! I heard you speak at..." and a long conversation about bridge began.

Cicely pretended to listen as she sipped her champagne, and surreptitiously watched Mark and the press of people around him. Maybe she wouldn't get to speak to him at all. But if she did, she would be calm and pleasant and—

A stab of pain shot through her as she saw a blond head lean in front of Mark to speak to someone else. Crystal! Of course. Cicely wasn't surprised; she'd known that Crystal would be by his side. But suddenly she was gripped by a hot flash of anger. Crystal was acting as if she owned him, her hand possessively on his arm, nodding graciously at everyone who approached him. As if she had a right to be there, to accept compliments for him!

The pain and the anger seemed to merge and explode into such a torment of agony that Cicely wanted to run from the room. She glanced around for some means of escape.

"Cicely, would you come with me for a moment? I want to ask you something." Grateful for the interruption, Cicely tried to compose herself as she followed Lisa from the room.

"I've been grinning and talking for the past three hours, and now I'm worn out," Lisa said, leading Cicely up the stairs and down a long, quiet hall to her bedroom. "I staggered the guests, you know, and you were among the last group to arrive." Cicely glanced admiringly around the room, done in rich tones of beige and brown, while Lisa paused before a full-length mirror. "Oh, Cicely, I do love this dress! Mark bought it for me, you know."

"Mark?" Cicely was unable to conceal her surprise.

"Yes, he gave me a check and told me to go to this shop in Roseville, and . . . well, when I came home in raptures, he told me that someone he knew had designed it. Later on, of course, I suspected who that someone was and wormed the truth out of him. Oh, sit on the chaise and rest for a few minutes." Lisa kicked off her shoes and settled comfortably on the bed, leaning against a pile of pillows. "I don't think we'll be missed for a little while."

"And he never said one word," Cicely murmured more to herself than to Lisa, as she remembered what the sale of that dress had meant to her. Had Mark realized then how much she'd needed the money? "Mark is so caring about . . . about people," she said.

"Yes, and some women take advantage of that caring and they use it to insinuate themselves. You see, in some ways, Mark is so innocent and unsuspecting. Not to mention attractive. And wealthy!" she added, giving Cicely a significant look. "There were several women in England . . . well, I'm pretty sure they had their eyes on the manor house more than on Mark. Which is one reason I dragged him over here to finish that book. And I made him promise to conceal his identity while he was here."

"Oh, so that's why you didn't tell me . . ."

"You must forgive me, Cicely. I didn't tell you that day who and what he really was, because I just didn't want it to get out! As soon as people find out about his money . . . And as you can see, it's happening again. Case in point: Crystal Morris!"

"Crystal? I thought perhaps..." Cicely faltered. "Well, I saw them together in New York."

"Oh, they were just there to see his publisher. Crystal's promoting his book. Just between you and me, though, I think that what she's really promoting is herself. Since she found out who he is, she's been all over him like a coat of paint." Lisa broke off for a moment. "Oh, my. That does sound catty, doesn't it? And I don't mean to be. Forget I said it, Cicely."

"Of course."

"I know I'm just being an overprotective older sister. But Mark deserves a woman who really cares for him, don't you think?"

"Oh, yes, of course he does."

"And I tend to get a little wary." Lisa sighed. "I know Mark is a psychiatrist and you wouldn't think... But he can be pretty naive about women. Really. And I'm always afraid some greedy, aggressive woman—like a Crystal Morris—will snag him before he knows what she's doing! Oh, I know I'm being silly...and a typical big sister. Running on for so long about my brother that I almost forgot what I really brought you up to ask." Lisa walked over to the bureau. "Look, I couldn't decide which earrings would go best with this dress. Now, I have these drops, but I thought the diamond studs..."

"Definitely the studs. The drops would be too much for that dress."

"That's what I thought. But I was sure you'd know. Thanks, Cicely. Well, we'd better go down. Richard will be looking for me."

When they returned to the party, a harried Richard hurried up to Lisa. "Where have you been?"

"Oh, just having a bit of a rest...and a talk."

Cicely didn't see the wink Lisa gave her husband, for she was thinking of greedy aggressive women. And she was looking at Crystal Morris who still clung to Mark's side, although he was now moving purposefully through the room, speaking to every guest in turn, bending toward each one with his warm smile. Lisa's words still echoed in her head. *"Mark deserves a woman who really cares for him."*

I do care. I love you, Mark.

Suddenly, as if he heard her unspoken message, Mark looked across the room directly at her. She saw his eyes light up, saw his expression of pleasure, as if he had been searching for her. He started to move in her direction, but someone called to him and he turned back.

Cicely moved toward him, slowly but steadily making her way through the crowd. "No thank you," she said to the waitress who passed a tray of hors d'oeuvres. "Thank you," to the waiter who handed her a glass of champagne. "Yes, a lovely party," to a woman she had seen at the tennis club. Now she was almost there. Nervously she took a sip from her glass.

Mark, who was still talking to the man who had addressed him, didn't see her. Crystal, who did see her, pretended not to. She seemed intent on urging Mark to leave the party.

"Listen," Cicely heard her say, "perhaps we can slip away now and—"

"Crystal, how nice to see you," Cicely said. Then, as Mark quickly turned to face her, "Oh, Mark, I'm so delighted that you finished your book."

"Cicely!" he said. "I've been looking for you. I caught a glimpse and then you disappeared. Where did you go?"

"Oh, just talking to someone."

"While we've been down here talking up Mark's book," Crystal broke in. "Now if we can get this kind of response from a prepublication audience," she said, speaking directly to Mark, "imagine what it will be like once we get the real promotion going!"

"From what I know of Mark," Cicely said, gazing up at him, loving him with her eyes, "I'm sure his book will sell itself."

"That kind of praise from you, love?" Mark lifted an eyebrow and his teasing expression reminded her of other things she'd said.

"That shows how little you know about publishing or book promotion," Crystal said crisply. "But that's my business. And I've already started. Oh, Mark, you said you'd show me the place where you wrote that marvelous book." She slipped her arm through Mark's. "Please excuse us, Cicely."

"Of course," Cicely said sweetly, moving to Mark's other side as if to allow them to proceed. But she managed to stumble slightly as she did so, carelessly tilting her glass to dump its contents all over Mark. "Oh, dear! How clumsy of me. I'm sorry. Here, let me clean you up."

Ignoring Crystal's gasp, Cicely took a tight grip on Mark's hand and pulled him toward what she hoped was the kitchen. It was. She hurried past a surprised waiter to the sink and turned on the cold water tap.

She couldn't look at Mark. She was too embarrassed. She'd wanted to be sophisticated and aggressive. All she'd done was deliberately make herself appear clumsy. And she'd probably ruined his beautiful suit, she thought glumly, reaching for a paper towel.

"That was a corny trick," Mark said, as she ran cold water on the towel and began to dab at his jacket.

"Trick?" She bit her lip and tried to look innocent.

"And you did it backward," he explained in exaggeratedly solemn tones. "If you want to get me away from another woman, you're supposed to throw your drink on *her*. Not on me!"

"Oh, I'm sorry," she said, now thoroughly ashamed. "I just wanted to get you to...to...to..." Her voice faltered, as Mark took the paper towel from her, and tossing it aside, pulled her close.

"To do this?" he asked. And then he kissed her. It was a kiss of gentle sweetness, touched with such passion and so much promise that Cicely's heart leaped in response. She wrapped her arms around him, and for a long moment they were both oblivious to the waiters scurrying past, casting significant glances and knowing smiles in their direction.

"If you marry me," Mark suggested a while later, "you won't have to go to so much trouble. All you'll have to do is look at me with those haunting blue eyes, and I'll come running."

"Oh, yes, yes, yes. I love you, Mark. I really love you."

"And I love you." He looked around, and for the first time seemed to notice that they weren't alone. "Listen," he whispered in a teasing voice, "wouldn't you like to come out to the guest house and see where I wrote that marvelous book?"

LATER, AS THEY SAT on the guest house sofa before a roaring fire, Cicely nestled deeper into Mark's arms, and they planned their future together.

"Of course," Mark said, "Alicia's welcome to go with us. Do you think she'll like living in London?"

"No. I think she'll probably prefer to stay here," Cicely said dreamily.

"Really?" He sounded surprised.

Cicely sat up. "Oh, Mark, Alicia is a different person. I wanted to tell you that you were absolutely right. That job has been wonderful for her."

"Yes, but..." Mark stirred and looked apprehensive. "First impressions, you know. She might tire of it soon, and—"

"Oh, no. She's not tired of it. She really loves it and she hates to tell them that she's resigning."

"Resigning?" Mark looked relieved but uncertain.

"Yes. You see, Dexter Diamond—he's that bridge columnist—has offered her a job as his assistant. And she's so excited. Well, you know how she feels about bridge. And Mark, I suspect there's more than bridge involved. You should see the way he looks at her!" She shook her head. "Oh, no, I don't think anything could entice Alicia to move away now."

"Well, well, well." Mark smiled with satisfaction. "Things do have a way of working themselves out."

"Oh, no. *You* have a way of making things work out. You made me have the surgery and send the sketches, and you made Alicia take that job. And...oh, my goodness!" Cicely tossed her head and stared at him in mock dismay. "How am I going to cope with being married to a bossy dictatorial man who knows everything!"

"Oh, I think you'll manage," he said softly. "If you're smart enough to walk totally blind through a restaurant full of people and pick out the man you want, I think you're smart enough to keep him in tow."

"I did do that, didn't I?" Cicely laughed and tumbled back into his arms. "And I was lucky. So very, very lucky."

"So was I, love. So was I."

Harlequin American Romance

Romances that go one step farther...
American Romance

Realistic stories involving people you can relate to and care about.

Compelling relationships between the mature men and women of today's world.

Romances that capture the core of genuine emotions between a man and a woman.

Join us each month for four new titles wherever paperback books are sold.
Enter the world of American Romance.

Amro-1